THIRTEEN FOURTEEN MAIDS A- COURTING

EJ LAMPREY

To Alex, who gave me Tenerife

CONTENTS

AUTHOR'S NOTE

This book is set mainly in Tenerife: I have not put the few Spanish bits in italics, as is customary, as it becomes distracting once the reader knows the words.

The Grasshopper Lawns characters are, of course, Scottish. Beyond the soft burr of the accents, which will have to wait for the audio version, there are words unique to the country – however, it rarely arises in this book. The general meaning should always be clear from the context – a brief glossary has been added at the end for easy reference to both Scottish and Spanish words used. Definitely is pronounced deffi-NATE-ly in Scotland and has deliberately been spelled '**definately**' in appropriate dialogue. The same applies to other spelling 'errors' spotted in dialogue (photies for photographs, polis for police, deid for dead, etc). I have kept this to a minimum, to avoid puzzling non-Scottish readers, but hope you will enjoy the occasional reminder that you are in Scottish company.

PROLOGUE

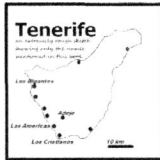

The young Spaniard spoke fluent heavily-accented English and was already talking as he took his seat in front of the big desk. 'He's taken the bait, señor. I have the dates for you.'

'About time.' The view through the huge window was dominated by the slope of mountain against an intensely blue sky, but the room itself was unlit and the big man behind the desk was silhouetted against the light, his features shadowed. His bald head gleamed, he wore a long-sleeved formal shirt, and his hands on the desk were beautifully manicured. The watch on his wrist, just visible under the cuff of the shirt, would have paid the Spaniard's salary for a year, and his voice had a trace of Scottish accent.

'I'm sorry it took so long, señor. It took time to find an angle that would work.' The Spaniard was slightly reproachful. 'Even the best magician can't force a card on someone who won't look at the pack. You said it had to be absolutely above suspicion.'

'Yes, I did. Is it?'

'Si, señor. I advertised the apartment online, a special for July only, with the photographs. It isn't possible to get an apartment like that for less than five hundred euros a week, even in July. Then I sent an email direct with the website link, special offer, romantic apartment, cheap flights from Edinburgh, only three hundred euros all in. Too good to turn down. I made it look like a general offer, of course. The only thing anyone could suspect is how they got onto a marketing list, and half of us wonder that.'

The older man nodded, grimly amused. 'How many applications did you get from the website?'

'For that apartment? At a special, even unspecified, price?' The Spaniard rolled his eyes. 'Nearly a thousand hits on the website. Over two hundred enquiries. I was very pleased when he took the bait; one more day and I would have had to take it offline anyway, it was driving me loco.'

'Huh. You were paid enough. Give me the dates.' He glanced at the paper pushed across the table, then flicked through a desk diary. 'Do it on the Thursday night. She'll call for help the next day, right? And Friday's good for me.'

'I can't see how she wouldn't. As far as I can establish, she doesn't speak Spanish so she'll be in a panic.'

'Good. That's it, then. Operation *Déjà Vu*. This should be interesting.'

PART ONE - GOING, GOING

MYSTERY MAN

The main house, three storeys high and designed to resemble a small but rather pleasing country mansion, glistened in the persistent drizzle. Many of the bungalow units branching from it to enclose the enormous lawn had their lights on, despite it being the middle of the day. Grasshopper Lawns, a retirement village for interesting single people over the age of fifty-five, looked deserted. Most of the residents would normally, as the summer slid into July, have been actively gardening, squabbling over the boules courts or playing croquet and generally enjoying glorious sunshine, but the Scottish weather wasn't getting with the programme. The campsite across the road, mainly for family visitors, had a scattering of caravans and even the occasional soggy tent, but even there the only sign of life was two glum dog-walkers trudging dutifully into the distance while their damp dogs cast wistful glances back at the Lawns. The small row of shops at the top of the campsite was bravely lit, and the end one, its window emblazoned **Rainy Days And Sundays**, was enjoying more custom than usual.

Those visitors not eager for its offerings of billiards, books, DVDs, model trains and jigsaws had the alternative of going into Edinburgh, half an hour away, or to the closer neighbouring towns, Linlithgow and Onderness, to find distraction until the sun relented and reappeared. Taking lively youngsters into the main house was slightly frowned upon; the individual apartments were comfortable and, for their single occupants, spacious, but not ideal for any entertaining other than neighbourly cups of coffee.

Edge Cameron put down her coffee cup, glanced at her watch and pushed back her chair, getting up from Olga's kitchen table with a little exclamation of dismay.

'Olga, look at the time! You said you had something on at one, and it's nearly that now! I'll get out of your way.'

She and the retired ballerina had been neighbours for nearly four years without becoming close friends but they enjoyed each other's company. Edge didn't often do the double exercise class at the Lawns but when she did, they invariably had coffee together afterwards.

In the last year they had usually been joined by Donald and Jayenthi, who both, like Olga, took the double session every day. Today, however, Jayenthi was away on holiday and Donald had excused himself almost immediately. The luxury of an uninterrupted blether had engrossed both women and Edge hurriedly took her leave over Olga's token protest, only realizing when she reached her own apartment door that she had mislaid her keys. She muttered crossly under her breath and tried her window, left ajar for the cat, a little dubiously.

It opened another inch, then stopped as the safety catch locked. A malicious gust of wind blew drizzle under the covered walkway.

'*Blast*!' She jiggled from foot to foot, three cups of coffee suddenly making themselves felt. Nothing for it but to go back. She sighed, turned on her heel and returned to Olga's studio apartment, turning the handle and opening the door even as she called out, 'Knock, knock, me again! I'm sorry but I've lost my keys, and I really need your loo!'

Olga, still at the kitchen table, twisted round, surprised, from her laptop and tried to block the screen with her body, but not in time to stop Edge glimpsing a heavy-featured man of around their age looking startled and not best pleased at the interruption.

'I'm so sorry,' Edge repeated, averting her eyes instantly. 'I've lost my keys and I'm bursting!'

'Of course, go to the bathroom, I vill find your keys.' Olga stood up smoothly, fully blocking the screen and Edge hurried past, a grin tugging at her lips. The mystery lover!

She was still smiling as she washed her hands a few moments later and deftly tucked a strand of her red-blonde hair back into the French plait she preferred for the exercise class. She was attractive, gracefully mature and at ease with her appearance, but Olga Petrotchovich had been beautiful by any standards when, as a rising star in the Russian ballet corps, she had defected to the UK. She remained timelessly beautiful now, in her early sixties, and she would doubtless still be beautiful at eighty. Two or three times a year she disappeared quietly on holiday with a 'friend'. Rumour at the Lawns persisted that he was the diplomat who had assisted her defection, but she could never be drawn on the subject.

Much as Edge would love another glimpse, she flushed the lavatory in as marked a manner as she could and rattled the bathroom doorknob before emerging sedately. Olga was still at the table, but the screen now showed her Facebook page and the calm oval of her face was enigmatic.

'I found your keys. They had slipped out of your handbag onto the mat.' She held them out and Edge took them gratefully.

'Phew, I would have hated to search every inch between here and the main house. I'm so sorry I barged in.'

'I vill teach you some exercises you can do to strengthen your bladder control.' Olga smiled, though, as she said it and glanced at the computer screen. 'But not now.'

'No, I got that.' Edge smiled back. 'I didn't see. Not clearly, anyway.'

'Good.' Olga's eyes creased with sudden mischief. 'I vill be avay on holiday soon. Nice and quiet for you, no neighbour next door.'

—ele—

'More an impression than a clear look. He was dark, our age,' Edge told Donald MacDonald slightly regretfully. They were in his apartment because the weekly cleaning service was busy doing their monthly thorough clean in hers. 'Bald, tanned, quite a broad face. A strong nose. That was all I could see.'

'You'd be a rubbish spy.' He brought coffee over, nudged his whippet out of the way, and sank down next to her on his enormous leather sofa. An unusually good-looking man with vivid blue eyes, he had been her friend for some eighteen months, for the first year of which she had believed he was gay. Some six months earlier that had changed, in rather dramatic circumstances, and they had been virtually inseparable ever since. 'A broad face does sound Slavic. On the other hand, anyone who was a senior diplomat forty years ago would be looking quite tatty by now. Maybe she's doing some online dating.'

'Oh no, she had all her clothes on,' Edge said vaguely and Donald threw his head back in one of his rare shouts of laughter.

'What does *that* mean?'

Edge was slightly defensive. 'Well, webcams—isn't it all cybersex?'

'*No*, you numpty. I Skyped for years without so much as loosening my top button. And Vivian talks to her grandkids in South Africa on her webcam. Pretty sure they are all fully dressed throughout. Where on earth did you get such an odd idea? Okay, perhaps *some* couples stretch the boundaries a bit. The same couples who send each other naughty photies. That's like saying because your mobile phone can take photographs, you must be permanently sending snaps of your bits. You've never sent *me* any.' His eyes gleamed and he opened his mouth again. Edge promptly covered it with her hand.

'Don't even *think* it. And don't mock me, I'm the singles expert, remember? One of those singles websites I was on had a chat room. The only time I went in, one guy was complaining that women didn't seem to understand that they were *expected* to flash their boobs on Skype. He was shouted down by some people but others were agreeing.'

His eyes creased with laughter over her hand, and he plucked it away firmly to wrap it around her coffee cup. 'I treasure you, Miss Prim. We need to invite Olga to join us in the house pub for a drink tonight, grill her about this bloke. You've slightly worried me with the idea she could be meeting strangers. You of all people know how dangerous it can be.'

'Good luck with that, you know how tight-lipped she is.' Edge glanced out of the window and sighed. 'She's away on holiday soon, she said. Lucky woman. I usually love July but I'm beginning to wonder if the summer will *ever* kick into gear.'

VIVIAN IS BLUE

TUESDAY

'I really like it,' Edge said for the second time and Vivian Oliver turned slightly reluctantly from the mirror over her fireplace, her lovely smile lighting her face.

'It *is* good, isn't it? I needed a cheer-up. I had to have one of the young hairdressers today and I threatened her with death if she gave me old-lady curls. I think I scared her, but it's the best cut I've had in *years*. I absolutely hate it when they ruin the whole thing by turning you into a beautifully coiffed granny.'

'You *are* a granny.' Edge couldn't resist and Vivian pulled a face at her. 'No, I know exactly what you mean. When I have anyone but Andre for my streaks they pull dubious faces and suggest it's time I cut my hair short. Easier at *my age*.' She snorted and raised a hand to touch her hair, pulled today into a practical twist. The hair in question was abundant and shoulder-length when it was down, but usually piled up into one of the variety of casual styles she favoured. 'The day someone offers me a blue rinse is the day throats get cut. Mine or theirs, I'll decide at the time.'

'Be fair. When you were twenty-something, anyone of our age seemed older than Noah.' Vivian shot one last glance at her reflection and sat down, reaching for her half-drunk cup of coffee. 'Anyway. What are you doing about this wretched wedding?'

'Fiona and Brian? I had specifically told her not to invite me—too awkward for words, her marrying my old beau—but my invitation arrived this morning. You too?'

'It's offensively short notice,' Vivian said crossly. 'Six weeks! She's been planning the wedding for nearly a *year*! What are you going to say? She's your horrible stepdaughter, after all.'

The two women were having coffee together in Vivian's studio apartment. The weather still hadn't relented, and rain lashed against the windows. Vivian, tall and well-rounded, was resplendent in a slightly baggy poppy-red jersey suit which clashed cheerfully with her nicely-cut hair, while Edge was slender in a bottle-green knitted suit which Donald had picked out, lightly made-up and indefinably elegant. Despite their differences the two women had been close friends for fifty years.

'I haven't decided yet.' Edge cradled her cup in her hands, frowning slightly. 'Donald has a part-share in a villa which isn't that far from Mercia, and he'll check if he can swap times with one of the other owners. If it's available, he'd like us to go. He loves Spain, you know that. Any excuse, as far as he's concerned. And Fiona did put in a covering note apologizing for the late invitation. Didn't she with yours?'

'Oh, something about how happy she'd be if I could, but she knew it would be difficult. And I absolutely mustn't think the invitation was a ploy for a wedding present, it was a genuine wish that someone she had known so well as a child could share the day with her. *Tosh*. And William is fed up too; she sent to the invitation to me and said I was more than welcome to bring someone. She knows perfectly well that he's the only someone in my life! It was just rude. He took the huff a bit. Said I could take anyone I liked but *he* doesn't fly in city hoppers.'

Her lovely smile flickered briefly at the memory. 'Apparently the first time he realized he'd have to squeeze even to get up the *steps* to a plane, he turned back on the spot. He hasn't flown since. The only way I could talk him into South Africa for next winter was to promise him that the intercontinental planes are bigger. He's still researching cruises.'

Edge grinned appreciatively. William Robertson was taller, broader and rounder than most men, an enormous man with a look of Holbein's Henry VIII, and held strong views. She drank the last of her coffee and tried to free her feet from under Buster's sleeping head. The old Labrador snorted, grumbled softly under his breath and shifted.

'I tend to agree with him.' Vivian topped up her coffee, reached for Edge's cup, and put the cafetière back when Edge shook her head. 'I hate that look on people's faces when they realize I've got the seat next to them. I'm not *that* big, or I don't feel I am, but modern plane seats are built for *whippets*. The more obese the Western world gets, the narrower they make the seats. I'm reaching the point where I hate flying too. Edge, don't leave yet. Unless you're absolutely rushing?'

'No rush. Is something wrong? You've not been your usual cheerful self but I haven't liked to ask.'

'Nothing wrong, *per se*. But out of sorts, yes. I don't like being at outs with William, for one thing, and we've been arguing over the whole referendum thing. I'm entitled to my opinion, and if my opinion is that we're better staying as part of the UK, and he's gone all starry-eyed about independence, that shouldn't be an issue, should it? It's only politics, and he's always been scathing about politics. Says that every government is just a figurehead for the powers that really run things. Suddenly that's all changed.'

'Well, accept the invitation, then. If Donald can get the villa, we can escape a lot of the jostling and agitations. The timing is perfect. Anyway, you used to love Spain. Your father was posted there for about four years, wasn't he? I remember visiting you at least twice in Madrid.'

'Yes, I loved it, but not in August! I'd *melt*. I haven't cared for Fiona since her behaviour over the whole Brian thing last year, I don't care whether they get married or not, and I don't understand why you are even considering going. I don't seem to be in step with anyone at the moment. It's very close to your birthday—would you celebrate here or in Spain?'

'I'm not celebrating at all.' Edge was decisive. 'Nobody believes you when you say you're turning fifty-nine. If we're in Spain, at least there would be hardly anyone who knows it even *is* my birthday except Donald, and he's already fretting about turning sixty in November and threatening me with dire consequences if I plan a surprise party. We're all in denial.'

Vivian didn't laugh. 'I don't know how old William is. He guards it like a state secret, and who the hell cares, anyway? We all live in a retirement village, and he's been here the longest of any of us, a good five years. If he came here at fifty-five, the way we did, he has to have turned sixty sometime over the last year. Who refuses to celebrate a milestone birthday?'

'Donald, for one,' Edge said briskly. 'Spit it out, Vivian. What's really wrong? You *know* William adores you and you're potty about him. Is it something with your children, or grandchildren? Niggling worries about your health? Are you sorry now that you turned down the chance to sign with the recording company? All of the above?'

'Some of the above.' Vivian sat back with a sigh. 'And the horrible weather. I don't mind rain most of the year but we've had a soggy summer so far and it's getting me down. And yes, don't even say it, all the more reason to escape abroad. If Donald can get the villa, okay, I would be up for coming. It could be challenging to see how much Spanish I remember, I used to be quite fluent. Part of my mood is that I'm *bored*. I can't even volunteer to help in the referendum, to be part of something historic, because William would find that unforgivable. Anyway, it only seems to be the Yes camp that is doing anything at all; the No bunch seem to be shrugging their shoulders and refusing to take it seriously. You've all got things to keep you busy. You have no *idea* the amount of reader mail William gets through his mailing list—SF readers are quite chatty types. You've got the excitement of your TV series going into production soon. Donald's getting more and more involved in that too, and I feel rather flat and under-utilized and old and surplus to requirements.'

'Wow.' Edge raised her brows. 'Talk about the blues!'

'Well.' Vivian was slightly shame-faced. 'That did rather burst out. Change of subject. Did you find out more about Olga's mystery man?'

Edge gave her a concerned glance but obediently changed the subject. 'Not a lot. Donald asked outright whether the man she's off with is the usual one with the island in the Seychelles, and she said yes, but this time they're off to the Canary Islands. He probably owns one of those, too. She's incredibly cagey about him. Donald has changed his mind about him being a diplomat and has decided he's a drug baron. Pity *they're* not going to Spain, I rather fancied the sound of that private jet they whisk off in. We could have hitched a lift.'

'Are they going around the time of the wedding?' Vivian looked interested and Edge shook her head.

'Not sure but no, I think sooner. I told you she was cagey! I'll chase Donald up about the house so we can let Fiona know whether we're going or not. As for William, we just need to make sure we book seats with extra leg room. No problem with those silly narrow boarding steps either, planes are nearly all linked up to those extending corridor things these days. At *worst* you pull from the front and Donald and I will push. Sorted!'

GUARDIA CIVIL, ADEJE, TENERIFE

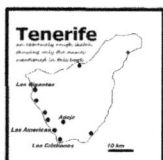

WEDNESDAY

Sunshine poured in through the windows and the air was hot, pushed about listlessly by a standing fan. The young woman was dressed in cut-off cotton trousers, a skimpy t-shirt and flat sandals, her sunglasses pushed up into her hair. She was torn between tears and frustration.

'Do you not believe me?' Her Spanish was good, but accented.

The younger policeman spread his hands. 'Señorita, what can we do? You tell us you went to a party at a big finca, you don't know where, with a man you met in a bar, and you only know his first name. While you were at the party you passed out. When you woke up you were lying on a bed, fully dressed. When you left the room a servant called a taxi for you to take you back to your hotel. You wake up this morning and come here to tell us, what?'

'I was drugged, not drunk! I had two glasses of wine, that wouldn't make me pass out! And the villa, the finca, wasn't far from Adeje, perhaps fifteen minutes by car to get there. I'm not asking you to check the whole island! I told you, I was dressed, but not exactly as I had been dressed before. Someone had opened my blouse, at the very least. The buttons were done up right. I do my buttons crooked, on purpose.'

She glared at them and they stared imperturbably back.

'Can you not understand? I was drugged and undressed at a party. Probably raped. Is the law different in Tenerife, isn't rape a crime here?'

'Si.' The older policeman was looking impatient. 'It is a crime, but to pursue it we must know there has *been* a crime. We offer you a doctor to examine you, but you say you showered before coming to see us. And who do you accuse? We must have some evidence. A name, an address, a start to our enquiries. Otherwise, it is an unfortunate incident.'

'A tourist making a fool of herself. That's what you mean.' The tears were winning, and when he shrugged she turned on her heel and stormed out.

The older policeman shrugged again and turned away. 'Coffee?'

'Still, this has happened before. A few times. Same story, every time.' The younger was diffident. 'Picked up in a bar, drugged at a party, interfered with.'

'With what outcome? We have checked before. Blood and urine tests show no trace of drugs. The ones who wanted internal examination, yes, there had been recent sex, but with a condom so nothing to suggest rape. No violence, not a mark or bruise anywhere: it must have been consensual. Different bars, different men. The barmen who remember them say they left willingly. They are never harmed, always returned to their hotels. It is not rape when they go with the man willingly. Far more likely to be spite, because the man disappeared. They are stupid, they learn a lesson, next time not so stupid, eh?' There was finality in his voice. The subject, it was clear, was closed.

DREW HAS A QUESTION

FRIDAY

Edge's ginger cat slipped in through the window and complained plaintively as she shut it behind him. Rain batted at the casement and was audible on the roof, making her cheerful little apartment seem all the brighter as she enveloped him in the towel she had left ready. Mortimer arched his back ecstatically as she briskly rubbed him dry and was indignant when she stopped to answer the phone.

She couldn't place the caller's voice for a moment, partly because he sounded so tense and partly because although she had met her niece's bidey-in often over the past year, they had never spoken on the phone before. She hesitated, puzzled, and he repeated himself anxiously, giving his name.

'Edge? Sorry, Drew McKenzie here. Could I come and see you?'

'Drew.' She smiled into the phone. 'I couldn't think for a moment who sounded so familiar. When do you want to come? There's nothing wrong with Kirsty, is there?'

'Nothing at all.' His voice became buoyant. 'She's perfect as ever. Would tonight be possible? She's on late shift, so she's not due home until past ten. I could come any time from now. Whenever. Or she's on lates all this week.'

'Tonight is fine. We're both in any time. If you come around seven you could eat with us? Dinna fash, Donald's cooking! Unless you'd rather speak to me alone.'

'Well, I would rather. But no, it's fine if Donald is there.' He drew a slightly shaky breath. 'I'll be around earlier if you don't mind.'

They agreed on six and she hung up the phone, still smiling. Donald, stretched out on her sofa, had rested his book on his chest to listen.

'Is he asking your permission?' He cocked an elegant eyebrow and she laughed out loud.

'You got that from what you could hear? Yes, I think so. I wonder if I should phone my brother and warn him?' She glanced up at her shelves, where a small clock kept Canadian time. 'They'll be up and about by now.'

'Because Drew wants to come round and talk to us privately?' He lifted his book as he shook his head. 'We could be jumping to conclusions. We shouldn't be hanging out bunting and embarrassing him to death.'

'As if I would! But I do think that's what it's about. He's rather nice and old-fashioned. From the things she's told me, he *courts* her. Flowers and little gifts, and treating her like a precious piece of porcelain. You could take a leaf from his book, you know.'

He lowered the book enough to grin at her over the top. 'Women, in my vast experience, prefer being swept off their feet to being courted.

And they've only known each other a little over a year. Very early days for an old-fashioned boy to be popping the question. I thought they'd be walking out for a few years yet. I shall withhold my consent, I think.'

She smiled, dried Mortimer's ears carefully and put him on Donald's abdomen. 'He didn't even really want you here. They're perfect for each other, you know they are. Want another coffee, while I'm up?'

He nodded, automatically stroking Mortimer and wincing as the cat responded with a flex of his claws. Odette, his whippet, lifted her head slightly jealously, then returned her nose to her paws and sighed deeply. It struck Edge as a very cosy and domestic scene and she was smiling as she opened the pantry doors which concealed her kitchenette.

'Would you like me to court you?' he asked her turned back and she glanced over her shoulder.

'I think that boat has rather sailed, dear heart. We're practically living together as it is. And to what end? Neither of us wants to get married. Apart from anything else we couldn't live here if we were, and anyway, you're hardly the flowers and soppy cards type. I like what we have.'

'So do I, but if you want me to be more romantic, it could be interesting. I might surprise you.'

'I've never been courted.' She paused reminiscently, the percolator in her hand, as she thought back. 'Both my husbands proposed almost immediately. James was *totally* unromantic. His proposal was, 'What do you think, old thing? Shall we give it a bash?' You surprise me all the time, and that's interesting. And enough. Anyway, talking of which, I told Drew you were cooking, but what were you surprising me with tonight?'

'Slave-driver.' He sat up, lifted the offended cat to the back of the sofa, and swung his feet to the floor. 'He may decide to stay after all. I'd better plan something which can be,' his blue eyes mocked her briefly, 'a romantic dinner for two, which can change at a moment's notice to a family meal for three. Is it *still* raining?'

'Still raining.' She put his coffee down on the side-table. 'And the weather is no better in Devon. I was talking to Bella Black earlier and she said it's foul down there too. They have to shoot indoor scenes only and it's thrown her schedule to pieces. By the time her current venture ends and we can start on *Pick Up Sticks,* it will be nearly November and even worse. Any word yet on the house in Spain, by the way? Vivian says she'll come too if you can fix it. Getting away from the rain is becoming seriously tempting. To hell with the wedding, any time you could sort it would be fine. We're going to dissolve at this rate long before August.'

—ell—

'I knew the first moment I met Kirsty,' Drew told Edge, his eyes unfamiliarly serious, 'that she was the one. The girl I wanted to marry. Does that sound unbearably corny?'

'A bit.' Donald answered before Edge could. 'But these Cameron women are like a punch to the gut. I knew the minute I saw Edge that she would be trouble, so I know what you mean. What are you planning to do about it?'

Drew flushed. He was in his late twenties with unruly hair and an infectious smile, usually concealing his sharp mind behind an engaging buffoonery, and Donald was enjoying his unusual formality.

'I wanted to ask Edge if it was too soon to talk about marriage. And if, really, Kirsty's dad was likely to approve of me. I mean, should I be going to Canada to meet him first? Kirsty's very vague about when he's likely to come back here next. And we *have* only been together just over a year '

'I said exactly that to Edge.' Donald was austere. 'Much too soon. Another ten years, and I would seriously consider giving my approval.'

Drew looked horrified, caught Edge's exasperated glance, and laughed involuntarily. 'Okay. Any chance you could pare a year or two off that, Edge?'

'My brother will be delighted: you have a good job as a paralegal, you're a year off your final law exams, but the *main* thing, you know, is that you're potty about each other. The rest is trimmings.' She bent forward, smiling, to clink glasses with him and sipped her wine. 'When were you planning to pop the question?'

He brightened. 'I'd promised her a holiday in Tenerife, and I had the most amazing stroke of luck on that—we're going next week. I thought I'd ask her while we're there. Romantic sunset, palm trees swaying, warm breezes, maybe a little Spanish guitar in the background, and, best of all, no police business to drag her away. But it *is* a bit soon, I know that.'

'It sounds idyllic. Go for it. What's the worst that could happen? She asks for a bit of time to think about it. Have you bought a ring?'

He drew a deep breath. 'That was the next thing I wanted to ask you. I have no idea what she'd like, she's not the sort of girl who gazes into jewellery shop windows.' He eagerly produced his mobile phone. 'I took a few photies of rings I liked. I thought maybe you could help me narrow it down. Just flick through, there are eight.'

Donald sighed and stood up to top up their wine glasses as she took the phone. 'Edge has no taste at all. I hope you've got rubies in there, for a redhead. You'd better let me choose.'

She chuckled, unoffended. 'No need, I've picked one already. The third one. Perfect. Rubies and all, Kirsty will love it.'

Donald took the phone from her and flicked back and forth through the images, then grinned and handed the phone to Drew. 'She's right. That one. Nice choices, I'm impressed.'

Drew took another deep breath. 'That was the one I liked best too. Wow. This is really happening, it's all coming together. Wait until I tell you the stroke of luck I had on the booking!'

——ele——

'Tenerife's a good choice,' Donald said idly after Drew left. 'I know people there, I used to go every year to visit. Same area, not far from Los Cristianos, where Drew's booked. It's an extraordinary place, incredibly stark and grand and can be as barren as a lunar landscape until you get to the next town or holiday centre, then it's suddenly lush and vibrant and beautiful.'

'I've been, but only to Santa Cruz, years and years ago. James and I took Kirsty and we all loved it. But I thought you always went to Spain when you went abroad.' She brought the empty wine glasses over to the kitchenette, where he was busying himself preparing their meal, and he flicked her a brief teasing glance.

'The Canaries *are* Spanish, numpty.'

'You know what I mean.' She was slightly annoyed. 'They're not that close to mainland Spain. You didn't say anything when Olga said she was heading there.'

'I was trying to get more information from her at the time. Anyway, I usually *do* go to Spain, to the villa. The Canaries have better weather in winter, though. I used to go around February.'

'And the friends? From the way you've always talked, I thought Seb was pretty much the only long-term friend you had.'

'Julie and her husband moved there when he decided to take more of a back seat in his business, must be about nearly twenty years ago now.' He was slicing mushrooms with quick deft strokes, not looking at her, and her eyebrows went up as she searched her memory.

'Julie? The one that got away? You told me you tracked her down, got her back, then got bored. I didn't realize you were still on such good terms.'

'Jealous?'

'Should I be?'

'*No.*' He finally looked up, slightly defensive. 'She was the only woman I had ever felt anything for before you, okay? We have forty years of history. That's attractive. So is she. She was devastated this year when I said I couldn't go; that I was in love at last. That's all there is to it.'

'Well, hardly. She knows about me but I knew nothing about your forty-year affair. I'm *not* jealous, I know how you feel about me, but I *am* a little taken aback.'

'Fair comment.' His vivid blue eyes searched her face and he relaxed fractionally. 'Her husband is intensely possessive. He believed me to be her gay buddy from her acting days, but the secrecy had to be absolute and it became a habit. I'm sorry I never mentioned it, but I didn't even think of her until the annual invitation came in, and then I didn't quite know how to say anything. There was no question of going, now or ever again, so I said I couldn't, told her why, and put it out of my head. You and I had separate lives for the best part of sixty years, there's always going to be new stuff cropping up.'

'True.' She topped up their wine glasses, a slight frown between her brows. 'I did feel we added to each other's lives, though. Now I learn I've cost you an old friendship. Does it have to be lost? No point in trying to make friends as couples?'

He suppressed a smile. 'She's not exactly my friend. She'd hate you. Her only interest in me, and mine in her, was climbing into bed to briefly recapture the past. I cannae see you sitting making charming conversation with Jack or watching him take his siesta while she and I slip discreetly away. You're a woman in a million, but that would call for a woman in a *billion*. Anyway,' he leaned over to kiss her lightly, 'I doubt I would be able to perform. I'm bound to you now, body and soul. Other women simply don't register.'

She grinned at him, nodding in appreciation. 'Prettily said. And I am certainly not a woman in a billion. I would be after the pair of you like a shot, breathing fire. Okay. Any other little secrets that spring to mind?'

He pretended to think, head cocked to one side, one wicked eye watching her reaction, then solemnly shook his head.

Los Cristianos

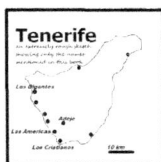

Tuesday

'This was the best deal *ever*.' Drew, wearing trunks and an unbuttoned short-sleeved shirt, poured himself a fruit juice. He went out onto the balcony to stare at the intensely blue sea, flecks of wind-snicked white against turquoise becoming lacy white fringes as the tidy waves broke sedately on the dark sand of the beach, or frothed against the breakwater of the ferry port. A warm salt-scented tendril of wind made the fronds in the balcony planter tremble slightly and there was a rumour of music from the boulevard far below until the breeze died again. 'I thought the photos must have been faked. A holiday apartment, how fancy could it be? This is *palatial*. Kirsty?' He raised his voice slightly. 'Wotcha doing?'

'Changing into my bikini,' she called back, sounding excited and happy. 'Better put your shades on, or your eyes are going to pop right out. Getting a professional spray tan was worth every *penny*. I look like a film star!'

He grinned, and slipped his hand into his pocket to reassure himself yet again that the ring was still there, in a special slim leather pouch. Propose now? Over dinner? Later in the week? He wanted it to be perfect.

'You always look like a film star.' He stepped back into the expanse of the holiday apartment, marble-tiled and cool white, with a single soft-washed abstract of the sea above the enormous bed. There was a chaise longue in colours exactly matching the abstract, and a low-hung lamp over a glass and steel dining suite, but no other furniture, just sculptural plants, spiky and elegant.

'Beautiful,' he said, almost under his breath, as Kirsty came out of the bathroom, slender and unfamiliarly bronzed in a cream, gold and black bikini, her striking red hair tumbling down her back. He swallowed hard and said it again. '*Beautiful*!'

Her tinted cheeks glowed and she did a model strut and pirouette, then put graceful arms around him. 'Do you like me all brown?'

'You look golden, almost the colour of your bikini. I love it. Almost makes up for the odd smell!'

She pulled a face at him and took his juice from his hand to take a sip. 'They said it was a biscuit smell, nothing too rancid. Is it too strong? I've almost got used to it already.'

'*Noooo*! I shouldn't have teased. I'm afraid to let you outside, I'll get trampled in the rush. Mebbe we should spend the whole week up here.'

She laughed into his face and kissed him lightly. 'Not a chance. The tan won't last the whole week, once I'm patchy we can hide indoors. For now, we're going out.'

'Like that?' He obediently reached for the beach towels he'd left on the glass table and she held up a floating scarf wrap that matched the bikini, slipped into it and stepped into low-heeled cream sandals.

'All decent. And ready to strip for action. Drew, this is the most beautiful apartment I ever saw in my life. It must be costing you *far* more than you said. It's years since I was here with my uncle and aunt, and Tenerife wasn't cheap *then*.'

'I was thinking that myself: what a *bargain*. But this isn't peak season, so I guess that's why, or a late cancellation, or the general state of the economy since then. Fate deciding we deserved a break. Who cares?'

'Who cares,' she echoed, picking up her shoulder bag. 'I just want to unwind, not think of anything at all and let the heat bake into my bones. Is your Spanish up to ordering one of those Canary coffees? I remember them from last time, pure sin in a glass.'

'Espresso with condensed milk and milk? My Spanish, señorita, is definately up to café leche y leche. And might even run to dinner, if you play your cards right. At worst we can point and look helpless. This,' he drew a deep breath, 'is going to be the best week *ever*.'

And you'll have your few days of total unwinding first, he thought as he held the door open for her. *No rush. This is the rest of our lives.*

PART TWO - GONE

GONE PLUS 10 HOURS - 07H00
FRIDAY

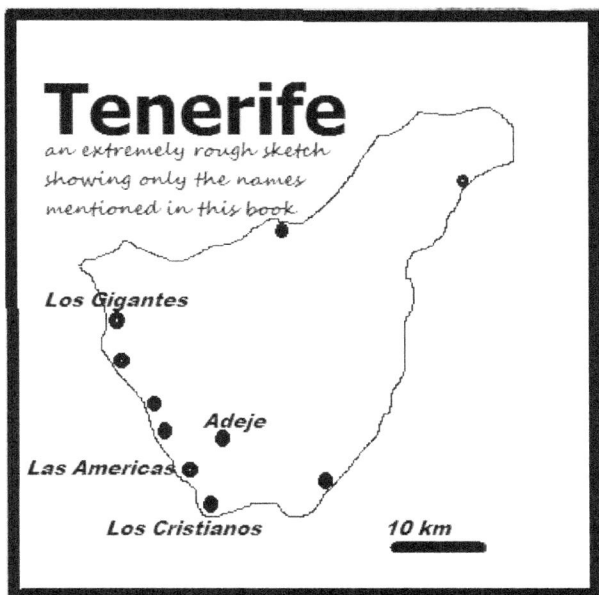

Tenerife
an extremely rough sketch
showing only the names
mentioned in this book

Los Gigantes

Adeje

Las Americas

Los Cristianos

10 km

Donald answered the phone a little sleepily, while Edge, not a morning person, grumbled and pulled her pillow over her head in protest. He tugged at the pillow.

'Wake up. Kirsty, and it sounds urgent.'

She groaned, rolled onto her back and took the phone, ready to make a pointed comment about the time.

'Edge?' Her niece sounded very far away, younger and uncharacteristically frightened, and she sat bolt upright in bed, sleep forgotten.

'What's wrong?'

'It's Drew.' Kirsty swallowed audibly. 'He's vanished.'

'What, just gone? When? Where?' Edge glanced at Donald, who threw back the bedclothes and padded off towards the kitchenette.

'Last night. We were at a restaurant, everything was fine, we've been having a lovely time. He went off to the loo and never came back. *Vanished.*'

'What do the police say?'

'Oh, the *polis.*' Kirsty's voice broke briefly. 'They have four different polis forces here, Edge! Four! I waited a while, of course, then asked the waiter to check the Gents for me. He didn't speak the best English so when he came back and said no-one was there, I went to look for myself. It's a standard set up: both doors in one hallway, no other way out but an emergency door. I pushed that open, and there's a sort of service alleyway which was empty. Crowds of holiday-makers on the boulevard at the end. I asked the waiter to call the polis and the Policia Local came, and they said to wait, he would turn up, this happens in Tenerife all the time.'

Edge smiled gratefully at Donald as he put a mug of instant coffee in her hand, sipped cautiously, then took a deep swallow, trying to kick-start intelligent thought. Odette hopped lightly onto the end of the bed, earning herself a round-eyed stare from the cat. Donald perched next to her, frowning as he tried to follow the conversation. 'What, people go to the loo and don't come back? Darling, I'm putting you on speaker phone so Donald can hear too.'

'Well, people get lost, they said. Lost! I told them I was a copper myself and tried to ask for the Policia Nacional or the Guardia Civil but they got a bit impatient with me. I'm not enjoying being on the other end of this, I can tell you. I'd phone Iain for help on the basis that a detective inspector carries far more weight than a mere sergeant, but until I can tell him which polis force will be taking it on, he can't put in a polite official request to give it priority. I *think* it's probably

Guardia Civil. I'm going to see if the concierge here at the apartments can find me a translator to take along, because they don't generally deal with tourists so they don't necessarily speak English. That's what the Policia Local told me, anyway. I *know* we don't leap about either until someone has been missing forty-eight hours but I can't seem to make anyone understand that he couldn't have got lost in a restaurant, and would never have gone off leaving me on my own. Never! Would he?'

'Of course not. What time did this happen last night?'

'About nine pm. We had decided to walk along the beach, then head to the restaurant for crepes. We found it on our first night, the most romantic setting you can imagine with a fantastic singer crooning love songs and picking away at a Spanish guitar—anyway. We got there just before nine. The thing is, he was a little odd all evening. Slightly tense, a little distracted. Then he said he'd be back in a minute, and went. It was about twenty minutes before I started worrying, and even then I thought he was maybe unwell, you know?'

'Could he have been?' Donald cut in. 'If he'd eaten something that disagreed with him, or drunk too much?'

'We'd eaten one of those meals for two around seven o'clock, and we both tried everything. We *were* drinking, but he's not a big drinker. We shared a half bottle of wine. He did get a bit sunburned yesterday, but it didn't seem to be bothering him. But he *was* odd. If he passed out I *suppose* another diner could have had him whisked off to hospital and the waiter wouldn't necessarily know: that's one thing the local polis said to check, the hospitals.' She paused to swallow again and when she spoke again her voice was a little shaky. 'I'm never, ever again going on holiday where I don't speak the language!'

'I speak Spanish.' Donald glanced at Edge. 'The flight's around four and a half hours, and it isn't peak season so we should get on a plane without a problem. We could probably get to you by tonight.'

There was a pause, then a gulping sound and Edge grimaced in sympathy. 'Of course we will, darling. Please don't cry. I'll send you a text with our flight details as soon as that's sorted, okay? Hang on, I just thought of something.'

She covered the phone with her hand. 'Your friend, Julie—would she know anyone useful?'

He shrugged, and reached to the bedside table for the paper and pen Edge kept there, in case she had a promising story idea during the night. 'She might not even be on the island, but yes, we'll try her. Get Kirsty's address. And she'll need to organize a local contract for her phone, or calls will cost her a fortune.'

'I already have.' Kirsty had heard the last bit as Edge uncovered the phone. 'Drew and I both did, in case there were any calls from work. Have you got a pen handy? I'll give you my local number.'

ee

'We talk on Skype, never on the phone. I don't have a phone number for her,' he said abruptly as they dressed hastily. 'Do you want to be there when I talk to her?'

'Not particularly. It was just an idea, you don't need to contact her if you'd rather not.'

'I'd as soon not owe her a favour,' he said frankly, 'but this is an emergency. '

'Yes it is, and if she can help she becomes my new best friend, whether she likes it or not.' Edge lifted Mortimer off the jersey she had tossed onto the bed. 'Blast, what do we do with the animals? I'd normally ask Olga to feed Mortimer but her place was dark last night so she's probably already away. I'll have to ask my aunt. She rather likes him, and he approves of her. Do you want Vivian to take Odette? Buster always enjoys having another dog around.'

He shook his head. 'We have no idea how long this is going to take. I'd rather pay to leave Odette in the house kennels and ask Katryn to organize a daily walk for her. Then I'm not worrying about imposing, if it does drag into weeks.'

She looked horrified and he tutted at her. 'Dinna *fash*, I don't think it will. He could reappear while we're already on the plane. Then we get to spend a few days away on a beautiful island without worrying about rushing back. Still, a man about to propose doesnae vanish without a word. Kirsty won't leave the island until she knows, one way or the other. You won't leave her there alone. And I won't leave you.' He smiled down into her frightened eyes and lightened his tone. 'Not until you can speak enough Spanish to get by, anyway.'

She smiled back uncertainly but tried to respond in kind. 'I'm rubbish at languages. That could take *years*.'

'Well, if it's *years*, I'd nip back and collect the animals. But not before you can order your own coffee.'

She frowned in thought. 'Yo quiero un café? I'll have you know I can order coffee in eleven languages. Anything more than coffee, though, I'm pretty much stuck at hello, goodbye, and thank you.'

He grinned. 'Don't learn too quickly. I'd not be entirely sorry to move there semi-permanently. We can get cracking on flights as soon as I've talked to Julie. Could you sort the pets out? And don't start packing yet: I'll do it, I know the sort of clothes we'll need.'

She caught his hand, suddenly serious. To strangers he was handsome but aloof, not easy to know. During his professional life as an actor/dancer and, later, choreographer, it had amused and suited him to adopt some of the mannerisms of his gay colleagues, and he was flippant and teasing with those he held close. Every now and then, however, the steel core in him showed through and it was immensely comforting. 'Thank you, Donald.'

'De nada.' He took her face in his hands to kiss her lightly, then was out the door and gone.

ell

Donald let himself into his bachelor apartment and crossed to his desk to boot up his computer as Odette, casting him a reproachful glance to remind him she hadn't yet had her morning walk, curled daintily in her basket. He clicked on Skype, found the icon he had never expected to call again, and took a deep breath as Skype bounced its signal against an old publicity shot of Julie looking glamorous and mysterious. The photograph stayed in place as she answered.

'Mac, darling! This is unexpected. What's up?'

'Not using your webcam?' Donald said wryly and there was a throaty chuckle from the speakers.

'You know me, darling, I like to look my best. I'm not rushing off to put on any slap until you tell me why you're calling, or how long this will take. You look as gorgeous as ever, but very serious. Problems with your wonderful new love-life, I hope?'

'No, not at all, but I do have a young friend in trouble and I wondered if you could recommend anyone who might help. She was in Los Cristianos with her boyfriend and he's vanished and she's panicking. She doesn't speak Spanish, and isn't even sure which polis force she should be dealing with; I gather there are four now?'

'Yes, there's one for all the islands, Policia Canaria, but I don't know myself who does what, there's a bit of overlap. Sure she's not overreacting? Men do vanish here, you know. Lots of very pretty women, and they can't resist temptation. There's not a lot of crime or serious drugs. He'll turn up looking sheepish any time now.'

'Maybe. So long as he does turn up. I know in Spain anyone who dies is cremated within twenty-four hours, I assume it's the same in the Canaries? We could be hunting for days for a man who's already ashes.'

'Oh, I'm pretty sure they don't dispose of *unidentified* bodies as quickly,' Julie said vaguely, then added with more certainty, 'who'd pick up the bill? It's an expensive business, dying, and even if he's carrying insurance to cover all the costs, that'll be in his name so there'll be a record. He just gave in to temptation.'

'Mmmph,' Donald disagreed. 'He was on the verge of proposing. She doesn't know that. He could have bottled it, but a man of twenty-eight doesn't leave his girlfriend sitting alone in a restaurant because he's had second thoughts.'

'Men do the most extraordinary things.' Julie's voice was dry. 'Why don't you come here yourself? I'll tell you what, Jack's son is flying here this afternoon in the company jet. If you can get yourself across to Prestwick by—hang on. Jack,' she raised her voice, 'when is Benjamin due?'

A distant voice answered indistinguishably and Julie sounded triumphant. 'Did you hear that? Jack's expecting him here by six. He won't be leaving Prestwick before one at the earliest, can you get there by then? I'll phone him and tell him to wait for you.'

Donald hesitated, then said reluctantly, 'That would have been perfect, but I won't be coming alone.'

'The mystery woman.' Julie went quiet for a moment. 'Oh, what the hell, Mac. Is it her kid? Bring her. Bring more if you can, a crowd would be more fun for me and less embarrassing generally. The jet seats ten, in absolute luxury. For that matter, the finca sleeps ten. We can put any amount of you up and be glad of it, we live very quietly these days. Do I have to be fantastically discreet?'

'I'm tempted to say yes, just to see how much of an actress you still are, but I'm too grateful. If there's room on the jet there'll hopefully be four of us. But no need to put us up, we'll find a hotel in Los Cristianos to be on the spot.'

'Nonsense. Stay here. Adeje is no distance from Los Cristianos and Jack will exert himself and pull strings if you're all under his nose. He knows pretty well everyone on the island.'

'Julie, thank you. I'll have to run it past Edge, but either way, thank you very much for the offer.'

Her voice softened. 'Darling, you're so independent. It's a pleasure to finally be able to do something for you. And I would love to see you, so I'm doing this for my own benefit as well.'

GONE PLUS SIXTEEN HOURS

13H00 FRIDAY

'This settles it.' William Robertson sank into one of the comfortable seats and beamed with satisfaction as he stretched his legs, wedged his walking stick safely into place, and shifted into position. 'No more SF. From now on I write porn. Prepare yourself for a lifestyle which will include travelling like this, my lovely.'

'I'd have no problem with that,' Vivian agreed. 'Does it have to be porn, though?'

'What do you think paid for all of this? Oh, Jack Rogers did some art films and some hifalutin theatre stuff, but it was the skin-flicks that brought in the dosh. Every other porn movie you watched from the late seventies would have been one of his.'

'I never watched porn,' Vivian said loftily, and shook her head when he grinned at her. 'No, honestly. You forget, I was living in South Africa from the seventies, and they didn't allow porn in any shape or form back then. You had to go to Swaziland to see any, and when we did go we went for the gambling. Which also wasn't allowed in South Africa. Ask Edge, if you don't believe me! We didn't even get *television* until the mid-seventies because the government said it would bring the devil into our living rooms.'

Edge laughed. 'I got there a year or two after television finally snuck in, but it was still only a couple of hours a day, half in Afrikaans and half in English. It was very pure, too. The only shows that got past the eagle-eyed censors were ones from the sixties bought as a job-lot, like the *Brady Bunch*, and *Star Trek*. Apart from the episode where Captain Kirk kissed Uhuru, of course.'

'No UK shows?' Donald was roaming around peering at the photos mounted round the passenger cabin. They all showed Jack Rogers with various celebrities. He paused to look over his shoulder. 'Oh, right, I forgot. The Equity ban. Poor little colonials!'

'It wasn't all bad. While the rest of the world was getting square-eyed, South Africans were focusing all their energies on sport. And we did get Dallas.' Edge shrugged, then smiled at him. 'I just remembered, it was a standing joke that the *Rocky Horror Picture Show* had been seen by nearly everyone in the country and was already at the drive-ins before one of the censors suddenly realized what it was about, and it was banned. Be grateful the NP aren't still in power. They'd only have to find out you used to tour as Rocky and you would be refused entry to the country. No question.'

'I hope I've lived it down by now. Considering our Christmas plans. William, you think you can churn out enough sleaze to buy us a jet like this before Christmas?'

William tipped a grand hand. 'Dinna fash. No sooner said than done. Someone pass me my laptop. That video screen. though; do you think I should do a bit of research first? Refresh my memory?'

'I doubt he stocks the feelthy stuff on his private plane,' Donald said drily. The remote for the big plasma screen was in a slot alongside, and he switched it on to bring up the menu of films available. 'Aye, mainly his mainstream stuff. Although *L'amour de Suzette en Rose* looks promising. There's a small private viewing room at the back, big man. Take yourself off there with your laptop and make notes.'

'Vivian would be shocked.' William sighed and leaned back happily. '*This* is the way to travel. May I ask, was the glamorous Julie one of his actresses?'

'No. He approached her to be.' Donald was brief. 'She told him to go to hell, so he married her instead.'

Benjamin Rogers, a broad-shouldered man with heavy features, balding and deeply tanned, joined them from the cockpit where he had been talking to the pilot. If he had heard any of the conversation he didn't let on. He was probably in his early fifties, his face barely altering as he smiled, his black eyes hard to read. To Edge's surprise he had a strong resemblance to the man she had glimpsed so briefly on Olga's computer screen.

'I'll be sitting up with the pilot; I like to be at the controls most of the way. I wasn't expecting passengers so I'm afraid there's no stewardess on board, but help yourself to anything in the galley. I bought extra milk when I was told to expect you, so we won't run out of coffee. We're fully-stocked with drinks, and there's snack food. If you're hungry, there's a small freezer and a kind of microwave thing, pretty easy to use. The weather's good, flying time will be around four hours, and I'll let you know if we run into any turbulence. Anything else I can tell you?'

'Thank you very much, Benjamin.' Donald, as the only one who had met him before, spoke for them all. 'We really do appreciate this very much.'

'Thank my father.' Benjamin stretched his lips again in his mirthless smile. 'Stick your head up front if there's anything.'

'Friendly bloke,' William remarked, keeping his voice down even when the cockpit door had audibly clicked shut. 'Damn. Think he heard what I said about Julie?'

'Not the end of the world if he did. She's his stepmother, no love lost between them. Better strap ourselves in for take-off. Watching us tumbling round the cabin might cheer him up too much.' Donald sat next to Edge and fumbled for his seatbelt.

'Does he have a brother?' Edge clipped her own belt into place. 'He's *very* like Olga's mystery man. Younger, of course.'

'Oh aye? He has two at least. Jack married young and Julie always refers to his first wife as a brood mare. She sued for divorce on the grounds of adultery and he had to be talked out of trying to counter-sue, as they all look ridiculously like him. He was trying to cut down the payment he had to give her—he's extremely tight with his money. Benjamin and his brother, Jim, work for him but not on lavish salaries or expense accounts, so no chance either brother would be sharing *la dolce vita* with Olga while they're on his payroll. Actually, now I think about it, Jim died in a car accident about two years ago. There was a bit of a rift with the oldest brother because of the divorce.'

He leaned forward to look out the streaming window as the jet taxied towards the rain-glistening runway, his face lighting. 'I love take-off. And then we can start plotting out what we can do to help Kirsty, throw some ideas around.'

'Count me out,' Vivian said apologetically. 'I'm always uneasy flying. I've taken a Valium already, I'll be asleep in ten minutes.'

'Check hospitals, from what you said.' William looked pained as the jet accelerated, then tilted sharply upwards. 'You *like* take-off? I'd forgotten this bit. I have to clench and lift, or the plane will thump back on its tail.'

He was briefly silent until the jet levelled out and he relaxed. 'Vivian speaks some Spanish, plus I have a writer friend on the island who lives in Los Gigantes, not far. He's fluent. Because of the rush to get across to Prestwick in time, I couldn't reach him but I left a message for him. Said I'll phone as soon as we land.' He glanced sideways at Vivian, who had discovered the seat controls and was absorbed in lifting the foot rest and lowering the back of the seat almost to the horizontal. 'I was thinking of the morgue. We probably need to check that, and there could be more than one. The four of us can cover a lot more ground if we split into two groups.'

'Fun outing for him,' Donald remarked and William grinned.

'He's not SF. He writes forensic thrillers, so he's in and out of morgues all the time, buddies with all the post-mortem lot. That's why I'm hoping he's available—perfect man for the job.'

'You have the oddest friends, William.' Edge was fiddling with her own seat controls but settled for raising the foot rest. 'How on earth did you meet?'

'Only actually *met* him once. He came to the book festival two years ago and we went out for a few pints. We talk a lot on Twitter, occasionally by email. Good bloke, very funny. Used to be a coroner himself. Bought a holiday home in Tenerife twenty years ago and retired there full-time a couple years ago to write bloodthirsty novels. What's your plan of action?'

'Translate for Kirsty, mainly, with the polis. Find out for sure which polis force we need, for starters.' Donald sighed with satisfaction as the jet broke through the clouds and into brilliant sunshine. 'So it *is* still up here. I was beginning to wonder. As for investigating, play it by ear and hope Jack really does have serious connections. I always got the impression he had the place pretty much sewn up.'

He glanced up toward the cabin and lowered his voice. 'Jack has always had affairs but he's insanely possessive. Julie was paranoid about him having her watched. It got worse when she lost her driving licence, and she was convinced he was behind that. She has one friend on the island he accepts, an elderly woman called May who lives in Las Americas, in the Patch. May was more sympathetic to Julie's situation than he realized, though, and she bought a small apartment in her name in her complex with money which Julie gave her. Julie could officially be visiting her but actually entertaining in her own apartment, and because the whole Patch is almost entirely British, anyone coming and going could get lost in the crowds. She still had to be careful for the first few years until he got used to the idea. Back then he had half the senior officers of the law and order agencies owing him favours. Hopefully he still does.'

'So why are we roaring to the rescue?' William asked curiously and Donald shrugged.

'He's fifteen years older than her, in his eighties now. Most of his original connections could have retired. And he isn't the most obliging man in the world. He's not going to bother about a total stranger unless we can engage his interest. That'll be Edge and Vivian's job, in a way. Charm him into helping. He was very susceptible to pretty women, hopefully still is.'

Edge laughed. 'We'll wheel Kirsty out. She's young and gorgeous and a genuine damsel in distress, so that should do it, no matter how old he is. Shall I make us all coffee?'

'She's out like a light.' William straightened up from peering at Vivian, who didn't stir. 'But aye, I'd go for a cup. And then unless we really have stuff to plan, I'd like to re-watch his one and only SF film, which I spotted when you were flicking through the list. I remember it as being so dire it was funny, but I haven't seen it in thirty years.'

Donald raised his eyebrows at Edge as she unclipped her belt to get up, and she shrugged. 'No problem here. There's nothing we can actually *do* until we get there, and I don't mind watching wobbly aliens in rubber masks to pass the time. Should I offer Benjamin and the pilot coffee?'

—ele—

Donald nudged Edge, who had been dozing, and pointed out the window. 'Montaña Roja. And the seatbelt sign just came on. We're coming in to land.'

'Impressive.' She stared out politely and Vivian, returning to her seat from the bathroom facility at the back of the plane, laughed as she strapped herself in.

'Red Mountain. That horn of rock. Donald, what are the giant slabs of concrete for?'

'They aren't concrete, they're banana plantations covered in netting. Fantastically built up at the front to keep them absolutely level. Nearly all the ground slopes here up the volcano or one of the mountains. Impressive as hell at ground level.'

The jet suddenly tilted sharply downwards and Edge, who had been leaning forward to peer out, swallowed and sat back. 'Damn, my ears didn't enjoy that! Where are my peppermints?'

Donald held out a tube of Polos and she helped herself gratefully, sucking hard as the jet banked and came about. Sun poured in blindingly through the porthole windows and she caught a fleeting glimpse of football-pitch-sized stretches of hessian netting far below before the jet levelled slightly. She had a brief impression of hundreds—thousands—of tourist apartments, white or pastel shades, extending up the mountain slopes, and then the wing was up and there was only blue sky and her ears crackling fiercely with the pressure. She shut her eyes, swallowed hard, and reached for Donald's hand.

GONE PLUS TWENTY HOURS

17H00 FRIDAY

Julie was waiting as they came through the passport checkpoint and Customs. She nodded coolly at Benjamin and offered her cheeks to Donald before glancing at the rest of them. Edge, looking at her with interest, was slightly intimidated: Julie was a decade her senior but so impeccably groomed and maintained that it would have been impossible to guess her actual age. Her figure was good, her skin beautifully tended, and her hair streaked silver and ash-blonde. A man would think she was casually dressed—Vivian and Edge, exchanging a flashing glance, priced her outfit at more than either of them had ever spent on a single ensemble. Julie dismissed them both with a sweeping polite curve of her lips and swayed towards William, smiling up into his eyes as he in turn politely bent to kiss her proffered cheeks. She sucked in her breath appreciatively, then stepped back to throw her arms wide.

'Hola! Welcome to Tenerife! I brought both limousines, but Jose could be a few minutes behind us. He was sent via Los Cristianos to collect your niece, Mrs Cameron. Would you like us to wait with you for their arrival?'

'How very kind of you!' Edge was genuinely grateful. 'And of course not, there's no need to wait.'

'No need at all,' Donald echoed. 'I'll stay behind with Edge, and we'll see you all back at the finca. If you don't mind, Julie, maybe your driver could take us to the restaurant first so we can get started on questions.'

Kirsty hurried up at that moment, looking strained, and flung her arms unceremoniously around Edge, who hugged her tightly. There was a strong resemblance between aunt and niece, but their closeness had its roots back to Kirsty's earliest childhood. Her mother had died soon after her birth, her father's second wife had been an indifferent stepmother at best, and Edge, who was unable to have children, had been stand-in mother, aunt, refuge and confidant, all her life.

'I'm so glad you're here, *thank* you.' There was a catch in her voice, and she hid her face briefly in Edge's shoulder, sounding muffled. 'Sorry, sorry, didn't mean to snivel. It's been so awful!'

'We'll help you find him, darling. I promise.'

Donald touched Kirsty's shoulder lightly and told Edge, 'Julie says no problem, we've got the driver for as long as we want him. Kirsty, where do you want to start? The restaurant, question the waiter there?'

Kirsty lifted a very flushed face and glanced about quickly, but the others were already moving away. She relaxed and concentrated on Donald's question.

'The waiter's Czech, his English was probably better than his Spanish, to be honest. The main frustration was with the polis. I went to the Guardia Civil this morning with a translator from the apartment block, but I'd ask a long question and he would only talk for a few seconds to them, so I *know* he wasn't asking what I wanted to know, or explaining the situation. They were sympathetic enough, but they're not going to do *anything* until Drew's been gone forty-eight hours.'

'Start there, then.' Donald turned to the driver who was diffidently waiting, and launched into a complicated conversation. Kirsty breathed out, visibly calmed by his obvious fluency.

'Oh, Edge! I've been frantic.'

'I'm not surprised, darling. Julie's husband apparently has serious clout here—we've got heavy guns to wheel out if we have to. You're not alone anymore.'

Kirsty squeezed her arm gratefully as they made their way out, heat engulfing them as they walked to the waiting limousine, dwarfed between tourist coaches. The sky was cloudless and deeply blue in the late afternoon, and palm trees rustled fronds above them, moving languidly in a faint breeze.

Edge drew a deep breath. 'Wow. I'd completely forgotten.'

'It is the *most* beautiful place.' Kirsty stared bleakly at the bustle of holidaymakers around the waiting coaches. 'Then you realize all the tropical flowers and green grass and palm trees are for the tourists and underneath is rock. Mountains and ravines and scrub, with lonely succulents. I loved it. Now I hate it.'

'And bananas. Don't forget the bananas.' Donald stood back to let them climb into the limousine. 'There *is* real life here, Kirsty, not only tourists. Real people, who will help us find Drew. Trust me.'

She smiled gratefully at him before she ducked into the vehicle and Edge squeezed his hand briefly as she followed suit.

—— eee ——

'Do you get the feeling they're ignoring us?' Edge asked drily as they waited patiently in uncomfortable chairs for the Guardia Civil. Donald lifted his hand to hush her, listening intently. There seemed to be only two officers on duty, and both were being harangued by a young woman speaking fairly fluent Spanish with the occasional English word as her Spanish failed her. Twice she seemed to swear but as their faces didn't change and she wasn't particularly emphatic, Edge guessed that 'fokker' must have a Spanish meaning, although she found it impossible to guess at the context.

'Another disappearing fella, do you think?' Kirsty asked Edge in a low voice and she shrugged. The young tourist seemed more angry than distraught, but both officers were radiating polite disinterest. Eventually the woman, sounding now completely exasperated, threw up her hands and departed, her cheeks flushed and her eyes flashing with unshed tears of rage.

Donald rose to his feet instantly and went across, Kirsty scrambling up to follow. Edge stayed put and watched their body language in the brisk interchange. It seemed to her both officers were a little wary. No, the hospitals and morgues had not been checked. No, it was not yet being treated as an emergency. Donald asked a few more questions patiently but received shorter and shorter answers until two men came shouting through the doorway. Both officers instantly switched their attention to the newcomers, and Donald shrugged, touched Kirsty on the arm and led the way back to where Edge sat waiting.

'Interesting about that tourist before us,' he remarked as they walked to where Jose waited next to the limousine. 'Seems she had reported being drugged and undressed, possibly raped, at a party ten days ago. She's been doing a little investigating on her own and thinks she has found the finca where the party was held. It must be a more common name than I had realized. Anyway, the polis told her they didn't have any record of her original complaint. They couldn't have been less interested. I thought she was going to slug the older one at one point.'

'There's no way Polis Scotland could lose information like that.' Kirsty looked slightly appalled and Donald gave her a wry sidelong look.

'Or the Guardia Civil. She was accusing them of deliberately losing it. Then she said they were being bribed and that she would go to the papers. *That* went down a bundle. I don't think she will, when she thinks it through. I gather she had no proof of any kind, which is probably why they didn't even open a file. But that's why I started by quoting the case reference you had, to make sure they do share records with the Policia Local, and asked them to give me a copy. No joy, of course, but at least it's definately on record and the copy is the sort of thing Jack's connections could get us.' Donald stopped short of the limousine to touch Edge's arm and point. 'Look at that sunset!'

'It's lovely. So what happens now?' Edge asked curiously.

'We could talk to the local officers who responded to the call last night, but the Policia Local are peacekeepers, not investigators. I don't honestly think there's much else we can do tonight except plan for tomorrow. The more we can rule out during the forty-eight hours we have to wait, the less time will be wasted when they do start treating it as a kidnapping. Julie did say Kirsty's more than welcome to move to the finca with us.'

Kirsty shook her head vehemently. 'No, if those guys are right and Drew could reappear at any point, I have to stay at the apartment. One thing to leave a note on the door during the day, another not to be there overnight. Please thank them from me, but no. As to what happens now, the guys I spoke to this morning seemed much more helpful and interested, even with that rubbish translator. He for sure wasn't telling me everything *they* were saying any more than he was passing on my questions word for word. They must work morning shift. I'd like to go back tomorrow morning, ask the questions that I'm convinced the translator skipped. Just the fact that another twenty-four hours has passed, they should be even more helpful.'

'Well, if you won't come to the estate with us, we'll stay with you. Or I will.' Edge was firm and Donald walked over to the waiting driver. He came back after a prolonged exchange, looking torn between amusement and annoyance.

'I told him we'd get a taxi back later tonight but he says he cannae tell me the address for the taxi as he doesn't know it! He's new to the island, and all his addresses are set in the satnav as locations. He goes where the satnav tells him to go. Can you believe that? Julie's always met me at the airport so I've never needed the address. All the roads changed while they were building the highway—we seemed to take a different route every time I came out to stay—so I'm not sure I could direct a taxi. Anyway, he's been told to wait and drive us around for as long as it takes. We'll see you get a good meal, Kirsty, and return you to the apartment before we head back. Or if Edge is really set on keeping you company, we can send him to collect our bags from the other limo, and stay over.'

'No, you can't, really.' Kirsty was regretful but firm. 'It's the most fabulous apartment you ever saw but it's just a giant studio with one enormous bed and nowhere else to sleep.'

Donald looked impressed. 'One of the penthouse ones? They cost a *fortune* to buy, and rent out at a thousand euros a week in peak season.'

'We're not paying anything like that, Drew got a really good deal. Probably a late cancellation,' Kirsty said vaguely. Edge opened her mouth and Kirsty hurried on, 'I don't want you to stay, honestly. I hardly slept last night with worry. I need some downtime to get my head sorted, and I *need* to sleep. But a meal first sounds good, I haven't eaten since last night.'

She managed a smile. 'We found a couple of really good places. No footie on giant TV screens or crammed with raucous tourists, I promise. Maybe we could even go back to the crepes place so you can see the layout for yourself. See if it suggests any ideas. I'd like that.'

GONE PLUS THIRTY-SIX HOURS

09H00 SATURDAY

The Rogers' finca was lavish and beautiful, flanked by more of the enormous raised banana enclosures which towered everywhere above the roads of the island. It was very much a working estate, with only a token frontage of landscaped garden, splashes of vivid orange, red, pink and white against emerald grass, and outcrops of craggy granite.

The four guests had each been given their own rooms, connected two by two with shared balconies at the back, looking over yet another plantation built up against the soaring mountain behind. They met for breakfast on a patio sheltered on three sides and shaded by a spectacularly-flowering bougainvillea which dropped Schiaparelli-pink petals onto a sideboard well supplied with breads, croissants, cold cuts and cheeses, a cornucopia of fruit, and jugs of juice. The centre of the display was two smoked hams on the bone, firmly held in ham holders with wickedly sharp knives, while an attentive young Spanish manservant—not, Edge noticed, the one who had waited for their late return the previous night—hovered nearby with coffee.

Julie, effortlessly glamorous in floating layers of coffee-and-white, was waiting alone and said briefly that Jack was taking his breakfast on his private patio with Benjamin. She asked how Donald and Edge had got on the night before, and how all her guests had slept, nodding complacently as they praised the finca.

'We do love it. The lifestyle here simply isn't possible back home. Jack was nostalgic enough about Scotland when we first bought here to rename the estate Seal House. There's a tradition in the family that one of his ancestors was a seal woman. It amused him to translate that into Spanish as the estate name, but we've not been back to Scotland in *years*. Benjamin and Jim do all the running around for him—only Benjamin now, of course. I miss Jim, we got on okay.'

Vivian offered a polite comment about the superb plantations in the sudden silence that followed and Julie shook off her mood and remarked that Jack had known nothing about growing bananas when they bought the estate, and had learned precisely enough since to hire a plantation manager.

Heat was already creeping into the day but the patio was angled away from the sun, which dappled the patio instead through a filter of blossom. A touch of sea-breeze from the wedge of azure ocean in the distance, which had two hazed islands rearing on the horizon, shook occasional petals onto the table. As lovely as the setting was, conversation was stilted and they all ate quickly, tense in anticipation of what promised to be a difficult day.

'I'll take Mac back to Los Cristianos,' Julie said briskly over coffee, 'but Jack refuses to be left on his own. Someone will have to stay and keep him company. You don't speak any Spanish, Edge, so you won't be of any use. It will have to be you. Or Vivian.'

Edge closed her lips on her instinctive reaction. They had returned late in the evening, and not seen their hosts who had, after all, flown them here and were putting them up. Kirsty needed her, but Julie had a point. There was also Donald's half-joking comment that Jack might need to be charmed and cajoled into throwing his weight behind the search; leaving him alone wouldn't be the best start. Vivian would have to be with William, even though he had reached Grant and arranged their visits to tanatorios and hospitals: he had only met Drew twice, fairly briefly, and, alarming though the implications were, wouldn't necessarily recognize him.

Donald was frowning, but he appreciated the situation as clearly as she did. 'If Jack has Benjamin with him, does he need company?'

'Benjamin doesn't live here. Jack bought the estate next door for the boys to share. Thank God. I loathe him and he loathes me, we avoid each other as much as we can. He's only here to get his orders for the day. He'll be gone before twelve and Jack will kick up a huge fuss if we're all out without him.'

Donald nodded, accepting it. 'I suppose you could wait at the holiday apartment.' he said instead. 'Kirsty doesnae want Drew returning there and thinking she's given up on him and gone back to Scotland.'

'So *she* can stay there then, let us do the running around.' Julie was impatient. 'She doesn't speak Spanish anyway. That's why she wanted you here, remember?'

He shook his head. 'She's a copper herself, she knows what she wants to ask. I'll just be translating for her. No point at all in her staying at the apartment, and at least you speak enough Spanish to cope with any official phone calls that might come in.'

Julie dismissed that instantly. 'The police have her mobile phone number, if they need her. She can leave a note on the door for Drew the way she did yesterday. You can explain to Reception, and leave a note for him there too. Don't be *difficult*, Mac. If we don't find him today, we can split up differently tomorrow, but let's get going, for heaven's sake. It's nearly ten already.' She stood up decisively and they followed suit politely.

Donald glanced at Edge, who shrugged. She hated the idea but Kirsty would be with them, after all, whether Julie liked it or not. She did feel a little deflated after rushing to the rescue and then being left to keep a stranger company, but the important thing was coordinating the most effective search possible and she was, like it or not, the least useful member of the group.

'So, stick with the plan?' she asked politely. 'Collect Kirsty and start with the police again?'

'I think so.' He looked relieved. 'I'll phone whenever I can and keep you up to date with how we're getting on. And I promise I'll support her as much you could have, okay?'

She nodded instead of answering, suddenly deeply uneasy, and he put his finger under her chin to lift it slightly and smile into her eyes. 'We'll find him. Whatever it takes. If we have to pick the island up and shake it, we'll find him.'

'I know.'

Julie fidgeted impatiently. 'Of course we will. He's probably returned by now and they're enjoying a lively quarrel. Mac, Jack said to take Miguel, he's the more experienced driver. And William, you'll have Jose. He's new to the island but both limos are fitted with satellite navigation: he'll find your friend in Los Gigantes with no problem.'

Edge returned briefly to her room after the bustle of departure, trying to scold herself out of her uneasiness. She'd stayed the night in Donald's room and intended merely to tidy up after strewing her room with the contents of her suitcase as she rummaged for something to wear in the pre-breakfast rush, but it was immaculate. Her clothes had been hung in the wardrobe or folded neatly away by some unseen chambermaid. She'd put her hair up hurriedly before breakfast and now brushed it out properly, re-pinned it and listlessly checked her appearance before squaring her shoulders, collecting her handbag, and making her way back to the patio to wait for her host.

Gone plus Thirty-Eight Hours

11H00 Saturday

Benjamin was with Jack when they joined her, and no friendlier than he had been on the plane. The physical resemblance between them was marked, but where Jack was utterly sure of himself and had a certain practiced charm, his son was an odd mixture of churlish and deferential, more like a difficult teenager than a man in his fifties running a financial empire. His attitude to his father was overtly respectful but Edge was convinced she caught a flicker of contempt on his impassive face when one of the servants brought a bottle of wine along with coffee at around eleven-thirty. The breakfast table had been removed and they were ensconced in superb huge basketwork chairs and sofas pulled round to face the view around a glass-topped basketwork coffee table.

The flicker of contempt passed instantly. The servant cleared the glasses and jug of fresh-pressed orange juice they had been drinking and was waved away. Jack poured himself a glass of wine and Benjamin busied himself with coffee for himself and Edge at the sideboard, bringing both cups over to their chairs in the shade, his face calmly attentive.

Jack certainly noticed nothing. Edge found the father-son dynamic increasingly uncomfortable as he issued a stream of suggestions and commands as though to emphasize his control over his son, half-glancing at her to check how impressed she might be. She sipped at her coffee, not reacting in any way, and was relieved when Benjamin emptied his cup in a single gulp and stood up to leave. She was strongly tempted to do the same: unlike the coffee at breakfast, which had been delicious, this was faintly and unpleasantly chalky. When Jack turned his head to give one final order to his departing son, she instead tipped the second half hastily into the ornamental urn next to her chair and was holding the cup to her lips to drain the dregs when he turned back.

'You were thirsty?' He leaned forward to pick up the wine bottle on the table with a grunt of effort, tilting it invitingly. She shook her head, smiling, and he topped up his own glass and studied her curiously from behind his sunglasses. She had been studying him with as much interest. Forty years ago, Julie had chosen to stay in her marriage rather than elope with Donald and Edge knew from the photographs that covered the walls that he had been a burly man of imposing bulk, dark-haired, rarely smiling. The photos showed him with most of the successful theatre and film actors from the 1970s onward, often with Julie radiantly beside him. She had weathered the intervening years better than he had. He was now totally bald, deeply tanned, still heavy and with a perceptible belly, but flabbiness around his jowls and his exposed arms suggested recent and rapid weight loss. His heavy lips, and the shadows under his eyes, were purple, but it was his expression which made him actively unattractive. It was hard to believe he had specifically asked for company, as he was watching her with a kind of sneering disdain. Even in the shade of the bougainvillea the heat was soporific and his features seemed to blur together as a wave of tiredness washed over her. She barely got her hand to her mouth in time to conceal a yawn, but he wasn't deceived.

'The heat here can knock you sideways, when you aren't used to it.' He sipped at his wine, his heavy-lidded eyes barely visible behind the sunglasses.

'I'm usually okay with heat,' she apologised. 'I lived in South Africa for years, and it never bothered me.'

'Really? With that hair?' His lips stretched into a mirthless smile. 'Perhaps you aren't really a redhead. Julie went red for a while. To please MacDonald, of course.'

Her attention sharpened abruptly. 'I'm sorry?'

'You didn't know? They've been lovers for years. Why do you think you were left here to keep me busy while they went off together?'

Donald had told her Jack never knew, never suspected. She gathered her thoughts with an effort. Shocked as she was, she couldn't shake off the creeping sleepiness.

'They've gone to help my niece. Why would you think there was anything more to it? She's years older than him,' she added cruelly and he shrugged his big shoulders, suddenly indifferent.

'It couldn't matter less. I thought we could have a little flirt of our own but you can't keep your eyes open. Go have an early siesta. I'll just sit here on my own.'

'Well, as rude as it would be, I think I have to. I can't understand it, this isn't like me at all. Will you do the same?'

'I'll be a long time dead.' He was markedly petulant. 'Catch up on my sleep then. Go. Don't mind me.'

She looked doubtfully at him, then bent forward to pick up her handbag and darkness threatened her vision. 'Whoa! I nearly passed out!'

He looked politely concerned. 'Stretch out on the three-seater if you prefer. That bit of the patio is always in the shade, you can sleep there. Unless you want me to get a servant to help you to your room?'

'Oh no, I'll be fine in a moment.' She bent for her handbag again and lifted her head quickly as the darkness crowded again. There was an odd look on his face, which was more effective than a splash of cold water, although his expression changed instantly back to concern. She stood carefully, smiled politely and went to her room on alarmingly unsteady legs. The minute she reached it she turned the key in the door, ran to the *en suite* bathroom and threw up, then drank most of a bottle of the water in the room's mini-fridge. Her sluggish thoughts circled round that expression on his face. Amusement? Could it possibly have been *amusement*? Because she was sleepy? Because she was—drugged?

ele

She sat abruptly on the bed. She'd been drugged once before, but that had felt entirely different. All she felt now was overwhelmingly drowsy, but that in itself was odd. She should lie down and think about it . . . with an effort she pulled herself back to her feet. Lie down, and she'd be asleep in seconds. She paced instead up and down the room, finishing the water and twisting open another bottle. The coffee. It had tasted odd, and she'd drunk less than half of it. If it had been drugged, she'd had far less than the intended dose, she could shake it off. But why would a man she had never met before want to drug her?

It was ludicrous, insane, but she trusted her instincts and always had. So, let paranoia rule. He had a lurid past, from what William had said, but he certainly wouldn't, at eighty-plus, want to drug a woman of nearly sixty for any perverted purpose. So she was to be asleep and out of the way for some other reason. She bent over her handbag to find her phone and her head swam again, but nothing like as badly as before. She had to squint at the tiny screen to find Donald's number, but the call went straight to voicemail. She tutted, and tried Kirsty's number.

'Edge! Where are you?' Kirsty sounded strained to the point of near tears, and she shut her eyes to concentrate, swaying slightly so that her shoulder thudded against the wall.

'Is Donald with you?' She already knew the answer and went hot and, as abruptly, cold. He wouldn't. He *couldn't*. Could he? The fear passed as quickly as it had come. Impossible—not that he might resume his affair with Julie, but that he would do it during a crisis. He wasn't in any way a conventional man, but he was an utterly steadfast one.

'NO! I've been waiting and waiting - he rang from the car to say you'd be with me soon after ten. It's nearly twelve, I'm jumping out of my skin!'

'Oh, bugger.' Weariness washed Edge again and she slumped against the wall. 'I was left behind to keep Jack company. Donald and Julie left before ten. And his phone's switched off.'

'I know, I've tried to phone him about four times. Your phone was switched off too. Do you ken her number?'

'No, and I can't ask Jack. He thinks I'm sleeping. Kirsty, I think—I think I may have been drugged. I've got a really bad feeling about this. Let me phone William and Vivian. You keep trying Donald, and let me know the minute you get through to him. But I don't think you will. I've been trying to think why Jack would want to spike my coffee. My brain's moving like molasses. Think of a reason. Any reason.'

'Spiked?'

'Darling, *concentrate*. It could be important. This is what we do, the four of us, throw theories at each other, follow up anything that could be possible. I'd think he did it so he didn't have to make conversation with me, for example, except that he had insisted on not being left alone. And I've already dismissed him wanting to make any dodgy assaults on my virtue.' She forced a laugh, and Kirsty echoed it slightly awkwardly.

'Okay. I won't waste time asking the how or when. If you think you've been drugged, I'll accept that. To stop you wondering why Donald didn't turn up? Or me being able to reach you to ask where he was?'

'I was thinking that. I even wondered if Julie arranged it for exactly that reason, except there was an odd smirk on Jack's face when I started flopping around the place like a rag doll. So the theory is that he did it, so I wouldn't be trying to phone Donald. Why?'

Kirsty thought about it. 'He'd surely not be pandering to his wife to that degree. Not giving them time alone, I mean. Anyway, if Donald wanted to be with Julie, he could fob you off easily enough. And he'd have given me a later arrival time. So Julie may be in on it, but Donald certainly isn't. To be crude, even if they *had* whisked away privately, not two *hours*, Edge. Nobody would do that in a crisis like this. A ten-minute quickie, maybe.'

'Been there, thought that.' Edge was slightly impatient. 'Think more. I'm going to ring off, get hold of William and Vivian, send them to you. With Donald missing, Vivian speaks more Spanish than the rest of us put together, we need her.'

'Edge, get them to pick you up on the way,' Kirsty said urgently. 'If you're right about the coffee, you shouldn't be left there.'

'I daren't,' Edge said reluctantly. 'We can't risk them being delayed here. Damn! I'll get away under my own steam. Anyway, I'll call you back when I know more.'

—ℓℓ—

To her enormous relief she reached Vivian on her first try. Her friend sounded strained.

'This is awful, Edge, Grant said we should start on the tanatorias with any unidentified corpses in case he's misidentified and cremated. I've seen two dead young men already. I'm not coping terribly well.'

'Lord, I can imagine. Listen, we have a problem: Donald and Julie have also vanished.'

There was a shocked silence on the phone and Edge shook her head crossly, as though her friend could see her. 'Don't try to be tactful. I don't think they're holed up somewhere. I think something's wrong, Donald told Kirsty to expect them soon after ten and that's the last anyone has heard from them. And I'm about ninety percent sure Jack Rogers tried to drug my coffee so that I wouldn't be worrying. Where's William now? Can you get to Kirsty and start a search for Donald and Julie?'

'Bloody *hell*, Edge. He'll be out in a minute. They sent me outside because the poor man they were seeing next was badly mangled in a car accident, and he didn't want me to see him unless he was a real possibility. We were going to start on the hospitals next. I'll tell the driver he must take us into Los Cristianos instead.'

'The driver?' Even through her sluggishness, Edge was surprised. 'I thought you were being carted around by William's friend?'

'We were, but the driver said he'd been told to take us anywhere we wanted, so Grant was happy enough to be chauffeured. He and William talk non-stop, they're getting on really well.'

'Vivian, that's potentially not good. If Jack mickeyed my coffee, and Donald and Julie vanished with one of his drivers and you're being carted around by another, he has us all where he wants us. I was asking Kirsty if she could think of a reason, but that's more William's area of theorising. Don't let the driver hear you, though.'

'I don't think he speaks English.' Vivian sounded shaken. 'Grant has been directing him in Spanish. I'll pull William to one side when he comes out. I think you had better get out of the house, if you can. At the very least get to the garage and see if the other car is back. Can you remember its registration number? All I can remember is that it was personalized—JR something. The one we're in is JR999, if that helps. And we'll collect you on the way, or do you think that could be a problem?'

'A *big* problem. Keep in touch. Dinna fash, I'll not stay here. Kirsty also said I have to get away, and you're both right. I'll call a taxi. I don't know the address, but how many fincas can have those ostentatious gold-tipped gates? The local taxis may even know it. Casa Foca.'

'Not foe-KHA,' Vivian corrected her helpfully. 'It's pronounced fokker. House of Seals. Are you sure you don't want us to come by?'

'Completely sure,' Edge was firm. 'If you do, there's a chance we won't get away again, and the main thing is getting to Kirsty and finding Donald. Be careful, Vivian!'

'You too. And listen, don't phone a taxi company direct, they won't understand you. Phone one of the big hotels. The concierge will speak English, and if you ask nicely they should order one for you.'

Edge sternly suppressed a rather despairing wish that she and Donald were still wearing Gerald Fraser's communicators as she rang off. Sometimes when you thought of someone hard enough they felt it, right? *Donald, Donald, Donald switch on your phone.*

All very well for Vivian to tell her to phone a hotel, but a quick search of her room turned up no phone book and her mobile phone had fairly limited apps. She suddenly remembered William had brought his laptop with him to Tenerife, but hadn't been carrying it when he left this morning. If she could find his room, she could use it to search the internet for a local hotel. Fokker. She had to remember the pronunciation. Something about it niggled at her, she'd heard someone saying fokker recently, but she shook off the distraction and opened the bedroom door a crack. A young Spanish servant lounging in the passageway straightened hastily.

'Señora?'

She blinked at him sleepily. 'What is the time, please?'

He spread his hands helplessly. 'Lo siento, no hablo Inglés.'

'Okay.' She fake-yawned hugely, shut the door again and leaned against it. Damn. Her room was on the second floor of the villa, with double doors opening onto a large balcony shared with Donald's room next door. There must be some way of getting down to ground level, surely? She was wearing one of her favourite crisp khaki cotton safari-style trouser suits, which would cope with almost any situation. She changed her heels for walking sandals, sitting on the bed as a last thread of dizziness threatened, and took her peak and sunglasses out of her big shoulder bag. No point taking that, it would only get in her way. She slipped her mobile phone into the pocket of her cotton slacks, and tucked her debit card, together with the few euros Donald had given her on the plane, into the shirt's breast pocket. Passport? Yes. She tucked it into the other breast pocket. What else, if she was going to be walking in the heat of the day? She fished the small water bottle she'd had on the plane out of the wastepaper basket, topped it up with fresh water from the big bottle, and slipped it into her other hip pocket.

~ele~

The balcony was even easier than she had hoped. A trellis, well over-grown with bougainvillea but reassuringly sturdy-looking, stretched up from the garden below and she took a deep breath, shook it a couple of times, then swung herself round onto it to climb down. It creaked dismally, and shuddered under her weight, but stood firm as she went down, hand over hand, as fast as she dared. She looked around as she reached the bottom in a shower of petals, getting her bearings. She'd hardly looked out this morning in the hurry to get to breakfast, just a glance at the swathed lush green of the banana plantation towering above the garden against the scrub of the mountain. How many staff did the finca have? No one, fortunately, was working in the strip of garden at this hot time of day. It was surely safe to assume that any staff, besides the youngster standing watch in the corridor, would be busy about their duties. Jack didn't strike her as the sort of employer who would let his staff sit about gazing out of the windows. If they were specifically on the lookout, she had no chance of getting away. No point worrying about it.

She walked swiftly along the house towards the garage, and reached it without attracting any attention. It was big, with room for several cars, but empty. Damn, again. She was about to leave when she belatedly recognized the five odd contraptions neatly lined against the far wall. Not golf-club trolleys with unusually big wheels, but personal transporters. Her sluggish brain refused to come up with the name, but she had ridden one on a holiday not long ago. She pulled one away from the wall and was peering about for its power pack when her phone rang in her pocket, making her shy nervously.

Kirsty sounded tense. 'I rang the translator to see if there was anything he could do to help. He couldn't get me off the phone fast enough. If we're going to be paranoid, I think he's in on it. Whatever *it* is. Did you get William?'

'I got Vivian but they're being driven around by the driver from the estate, not by William's friend. That could be a problem '

'Damn.' Kirsty drew a shaky breath. 'What the hell could a man like Jack Rogers have against Drew?'

'It's not impossible Drew was the bait.' Edge was absently studying the rack of transporters as she spoke. 'Listen, darling, what do you know about those upright transporter things? The electric jobs. I've ridden one once before, in Spain, but that was with a guide. There are some here but I can't find their power packs.'

'Do you mean Segways? We did a Segway tour the day after we arrived.' Kirsty sounded a little distracted. 'I think the power packs are built in. They were activated by a remote, quite small, that the tour guide kept separately. Looked like a stopwatch. What did you mean, bait?'

'Oh good, I see them, they're hanging here on the wall behind them with a schematic. I thought they were compasses. Hang on—*yes*, it's started humming. Anyway, I hope to hell I'm wrong, but Jack referred to Donald and Julie's history this morning when we were having coffee. He said it as though we both knew all about it, and that it was ongoing. I've been thinking: what if he seized the chance to send them off together, planning some bizarre kind of revenge? *Then* I thought he might have set this whole thing up to bring us hot-footing out to your rescue. As you said, if we're going to be paranoid, *be* paranoid. It could fit. It does mean Drew is probably being locked up somewhere safe, because you'd have phoned me immediately if he had been killed instead.'

'I hope you're right. About Drew, I mean, but that could be very bad news for Donald.'

'I know—oh help, now this bloody thing is trying to run away!'

'Careful, Edge, they're not the easiest things to ride. One of the people on our tour was mucking about, completely ignoring the instructor, and did the most spectacular fall! Do you even know how to get here?'

'Well, since Los Cristianos was clearly signposted from the airport side, I'm assuming it's as good from this direction. You're near that colossal hotel you pointed out when we turned down towards the town, so yes, I think so. How long it will take on something that moves at jogging speed I have no idea, but it should be under an hour. I'm frankly planning to buzz along the hard shoulder on the highway, and if the police stop me I will be utterly delighted. I just hope they are Los Cristianos police and not from Adeje.'

'And don't promptly return you to the estate,' Kirsty said grimly and Edge flinched.

'Damn. I hadn't thought of that. Well, if they do, Jack can't possibly confiscate my phone, can he? I'll phone you. When William and Vivian arrive, you can all come rescue me. This thing's quivering like a soul possessed, Kirsty. I'm going now. Phone Vivian and find out what's happening.'

BUZZING TO THE RESCUE

She ended the call, put the phone back in her pocket, and persuaded the reluctant machine to follow her through the side door back into the fierce heat before mounting it nervously. Lean your whole body forward to go forward, right? And lean back to stop or reverse. She leaned forward cautiously and the Segway instantly settled and moved smoothly forward, rounding the first corner of the driveway obediently as she leaned into the turn. The curve took the driveway into the shade of the towering banana plantation which flanked it, and although the change in temperature wasn't marked, escaping the glare of the sun was instant respite. She relaxed slightly, and realized a wave of relief to be finally doing something. *So far so good, Donald, I'm on my way*!

She had passed the deeply-shadowed gap between the giant raised banana enclosures before it occurred to her that it could offer a better escape route. She twisted back to look and the Segway spun obedient to her shift in weight, nearly toppling her. It fidgeted furtively, almost alive, as she swithered, trying to think. Follow the drive down to the electric gates, and hope they opened automatically? If they didn't, she'd have to turn back anyway. Chances were the gates were monitored by security cameras, too, and at the very least she would have some awkward explaining to do.

She had noticed similar narrow alleys between other plantations on their drive into town the day before, opening directly onto the road. There was the chance this slipway, or one of the crossing ones, would open onto the estate access road for the workers, but the equal chance it would lead her into a bewildering network of passages where she could get lost. She was humbly aware she had a very poor sense of direction and the wall of the raised plantation on the left, because of the steep slope, was ten feet of giant bricks, topped by at least another six feet of netting. She could see the blurred green silhouettes of hundreds of banana plants stretching away inside the netting on her right, but nothing else. She would have no bearings at all, but if she could find her way between the plantations, it would be safer than being spotted from the house—even if the gates *did* open. She glanced up at the omnipresent mountain. Her original intention had been to keep that at her back and angle downhill until she reached the highway, but it would be blocked from sight as soon as she went in between the high walls. On the other hand, the thought of travelling in the shade had its own appeal. She chewed her lip. *Donald, Donald, what should I do?* Presumably the passages were used by vehicles and trailers during harvest. They would be straight, surely, and each plantation was huge. How many alleys could there be?

The heat was, if anything, intensifying, and she was still finding it hard to think clearly. A tiny breeze eddied towards her and she turned her face to it gratefully, then froze as she caught a flicker of movement from the corner of her eye. The gates at the bottom of the drive were opening. If she had kept going . . .

A familiar black limousine nosed between the gates, the sun dazzling on its windscreen. The one that had taken Donald and Julie, or was this William and Vivian come to collect her after all? She leaned forward and the Segway slid smoothly into the deep shadow of the passage, then swivelled responsively. She'd had barely a second to glance at the number-plate but it was enough: JR007. Miguel, then. That ruled out an accident. Donald and Julie wouldn't have turned back without seeing Kirsty, and the car was supposed to be on hand for them wherever they needed to go, so they wouldn't have been dropped off.

She leaned back automatically as the car surged up the driveway and the Segway unnervingly retreated backwards further into the shadow. She could see into the car now with only the peaked cap of the chauffeur and his profile visible as the long bonnet slid past. No-one in the back or beside him. She waited, breathless, as the car checked, then accelerated smoothly forward and was gone. Had he seen her, caught the movement? The Segway lurched as she tugged it round urgently and headed down the narrow throughway, leaning forward to push it to its top speed, the need to get out of sight gripping her.

There was a recessed entrance to the plantation on her right but she ignored it, pushing on towards the cross road between the plantations and burled into it, heart hammering. The panic ebbed as instantly as it had risen. No shouts, no pounding feet. She fumbled for her phone with shaking fingers, absently brushing the back of her hand across her sweating forehead before she dialled Kirsty, who answered on the second ring.

'Edge? Are you safe?'

'So far, but about to get incredibly lost, I think. I'm trying to follow the tracks between the banana plantations. The limo just came back, without Donald and Julie.'

She could hear Kirsty drawing breath. 'Oh *hell*. I almost hoped there had been an accident. Edge, don't you *dare* get lost. Shall I get a taxi, come and fetch you? You could go down to the gate and wait.'

'We don't know the actual address, remember? I was going to phone a hotel, tell them it was the Casa Foca, and hope they know it.' She gasped and added breathlessly, 'Kirsty, I've just realised something. Do you remember that angry tourist at the Guardia Civil last night? She said 'fokker' twice. I thought she was swearing, but Vivian says that's how the estate name is pronounced. Donald even mentioned that it must be a more common name than he had realized, but I didn't think to ask what he was talking about. It could be pure coincidence but between that, and the return of the limo, I'm more freaked out than ever. I keep thinking I have to put as much distance between me and the house as possible. Phone Vivian, bring them up to date. Once I can get to a main road, I'll beetle into the first hotel or shop I see and get a taxi from there.'

'Stay in touch.' Kirsty sounded more like herself. 'I won't phone you in case you're hiding, but phone me every twenty minutes. And head straight downhill. You *have* to reach a road sooner or later. The plantations are huge, there won't be too many crossings. Is your phone fully charged? At absolute worst, the polis could track you on the signal, so let me know if the battery is getting low, you'll need to keep some back.' Her voice was bitter as she added, 'Tracking you is the sort of thing Jack Rogers could have organized in ten minutes.'

'I charged it overnight. Kirsty, you made me think of something else. We hoped he'd be a mogul with lots of pull, and okay, it's all in the wrong direction. But I just remembered Olga is in the Canaries, and her fellow is something of a mystery man, but *very* rich. He could perhaps help. I have no idea which island, but it *could* be here. Got a pen? Phone her on this number.' She reeled off the familiar number without having to refer to her phone's directory. 'Tell her everything. Any chance, right now, is better than nothing.'

Kirsty read the number back to her. 'She's going to love you. Isn't she fantastically secretive about him?'

'Yes, but she's very fond of Donald, and she and I have been friends for nearly four years. That may help. The only thing is;' Edge felt a bubble of hysteria pushing upwards, 'I think he may be related to Jack, even his son. He looks like him, and even more like Benjamin Rogers, who flew us here yesterday. I have absolutely no idea whether that will be a good or bad thing.'

'Wow. Risk him being so potty about Olga he'll go against his own father to help her friends?' Kirsty sounded doubtful and Edge shook her head impatiently, as though her niece could see her.

'No, they're estranged, they haven't spoken in years. He may not be at all—I got the briefest of glimpses—but it is possible. It could even be a good thing if he *is* Jack's son but on bad terms with him—the enemy of my enemy is my friend, you know? Up to you, darling, but think about it. I don't think things could get any worse, after all. I'm going to push on now. I'll phone you in about twenty minutes. One o'clock, make it. Okay?'

She took a deep breath, sent another wordless *Donald, Donald, Donald*, and leaned forward to send the Segway trundling at its best speed along the shady track

GONE PLUS FORTY HOURS

13H00 SATURDAY

Donald was weighed down with sleep, fathoms deep, but Edge wouldn't stop talking to him. It was really very inconsiderate of her. With a silent groan he cracked an eyelid. Light glowing through curtains drawn against the glare of the sun: must be siesta time. No Edge. Good. He tried to sink back into the billowing comfort of this wonderful sleep but she was back, less heard than felt, saying his name. When he tried to concentrate she slipped away again, was gone. Only a dream. He sighed and stretched out. Cool sheets against his naked skin. Nice. He reached for her, patted air, then his fingertips brushed her skin. Why was she so far away? It was hot, though. Maybe she had moved away to be cool. Of course it was hot. They were on holiday, in the sun. Spain? It must be, there were two men talking in low voices in Spanish. He sighed again and relaxed but his thoughts were stirring hazily. Two men talking? In their bedroom?

The radio. Or outside the window. Annoying, anyway. If it was the radio, he should get up and turn it off. Edge was a lighter sleeper than he was so it would wake her too. But if it did wake her, maybe *she* would turn it off and he wouldn't have to move. He really didn't want to move, he was as limp as a cat in sunshine. Resentfully, he tuned in on the voices.

'We should do it now. Get out of here.'

'I have told you. There must be no trace left in their systems. It can take up to three hours, and they got a double dose: the gas, then the injection. Patience, my friend.'

The other man grumbled, too soft to hear, and sighed. 'He is waking, I can tell. It is out of his system.'

'It can't be. He is dreaming, that is all. She hasn't moved, even when we undressed her.' He added, grudgingly, 'She looks good for her age, yes?'

'That is money for you. With that much money, *my* wife would look good.'

'So that is how you can spend your share,' the second man rumbled with laughter. 'I want coffee, damnit. This is boring.'

'No coffee. The smell of it could wake them. He has gone back to sleep now, though.'

Donald hadn't gone back to sleep. Although every muscle in his body was heavy, his sluggish brain was slowly clearing. These men had undressed Edge? Rage shook him, until the other man said '*my* wife'. A wife, then. A wife with '*that much money*' in Spanish territory. He rejected the obvious answer with another involuntary quiver, but he knew that window, had seen the sun on those curtains, had been in this bed before. He had never thought to be in it again, and Edge would murder him if she found out. Maybe she had sent these two men to murder him, because there was something decidedly ominous about their strange patience, their wait for something to be out of his system.

He had a sudden clear memory of sitting in the limousine, the driver running the electric window up between them. A hissing sound . . . he couldn't remember any more. Why had they been in the limo? He patiently backtracked through his memory. Julie flirting, looking petulant when he didn't respond when she brushed her nails over his thigh. After that. The big car running between the banana plantations of the finca, turning toward Los Cristianos. The sun-hazed road, craggy rocks and scrubby undergrowth replaced with bursts of colour as they passed white-washed houses dazzling in the sunshine, tropical flowers dotting profuse splashes of red, sharp pink, orange. Swaying in the back seat as the limo unexpectedly turned off towards Las Americas. Julie saying something, in a surprised voice. The electric window sliding up. The hissing.

So, they were in her tiny apartment in The Patch, but not by their choice. Naked because these men had undressed them. To take damning photographs for Jack to rid himself of Julie? Why would their systems have to be clear for that?

The answer was like a dash of cold water. If they were to die, the autopsy must not reveal that they had been sedated.

His thoughts were finally quickening. He concentrated on remembering the layout of the place. Saloon-style swinging doors into the kitchen, and Julie kept a set of butcher knives, good ones, next to the sink. He dismissed the thought—his reflexes were slower than molasses, he could never get to the kitchen in time past two alert men.

The apartment was tiny: one room with kitchen-diner, bathroom. Julie had bought a free-standing marble-topped vanity unit two years ago for the bathroom. She had told him, laughing, that it had taken two men, cursing and panting, to manoeuvre it up to the second-floor apartment. She had wanted him to move it closer to the corner for her and he had refused and mocked her for buying something so impractical. If it was still there, and still a gap between it and the corner, could he brace himself against the wall and push it enough to barricade the door? That left her out here on her own but surely what the two men were planning needed them both together. His safety would be her safety.

'Urghh,' he groaned out loud, his voice thick. 'Gonna be sick.' He rolled over, put his feet to the floor, and pushed himself into a sitting position, hands over his face. 'What I *drink*?'

'Stop him!' the second man hissed, and the first hushed him instantly.

'No, no, you want him being sick in the room? Clean that up? Let him make it. If he can.'

Donald lurched to his feet, staggered, and took an unsteady step, then a second, to the bathroom. Adrenalin flooded through his muscles, strengthening them, but he swayed more than ever as he half-collapsed against the doorframe, retched artistically, then stumbled through the door in the direction of the toilet, hearing one of the men snigger nervously. The door closed automatically behind him and he whirled and locked it so that the click of the lock was drowned in the click of the latch. No window. Damn. He had forgotten that. The vanity was there, looking bigger than ever. He splashed cold water on his face and head, with a noisy soundtrack for the benefit of the listeners in the bedroom, while he planned the next move. He could squeeze between the unit and the corner, jack-knife convulsively to push the unit across. If he angled it right, one push would slew it across the door. Then brace himself against it, his feet against the bath.

It wouldn't stop them, but they'd have to break the door to get at him and so much for passing any incident off as innocent after that. Especially if he thumped on the bathroom wall and perhaps roused the person in the next apartment.

It wasn't a great plan. It was the only plan he had.

PART THREE – Rescue, RESCUE AND RESCUE

GLASGOW KISS

William frowned as Vivian, her voice low, brought him up to date outside the tanatorio. Theirs was the only vehicle in the public parking lot, and there wasn't a soul in sight. Blistering midday heat and lunchtime between them had cleared the area, and even the dappled shade was hot.

'We're to liaise by phone with Kirsty. Edge is calling her every twenty minutes,' she finished. 'We can't phone her because she could be hiding and the last thing she needs is her phone suddenly going off.'

'Hell, no. And she thinks this Jose fellow is dodgy?' He glanced over at the driver, a powerful man in his thirties, who was leaning against the car watching them thoughtfully, his eyes hidden by black shades under the peak of his cap.

'Well, the other driver definitely is. This one's new to the island, we know that, and built like a tank. He might be brought-in muscle. I don't think we can take the chance.'

Grant appeared in the morgue doorway, looking a little pale, and William looked towards him, then back at Vivian. 'And Grant? He's local, after all. What about him?'

Vivian put a hand to her head. 'Oh hell. He *can't* be involved. How long have you been corresponding?'

'A few years, I told you. I think he's okay, but I don't think we can count on him for actual help. What's the plan?'

'Disable Jose somehow. Get Grant to drive us straight to Kirsty. Are we being paranoid? Maybe Jose would take us there himself. Not as if we're asking him to take us to where they're holding Drew—or Donald, for that matter.'

'I wonder if he knows?' William pushed his shades back up his nose. 'I cannae think in this heat! Hush, my lovely.' He held up his hand as she started to speak and she went obediently silent. Grant trudged towards them and she raised her voice slightly.

'William's feeling a bit off. Give him a moment.'

'I'm not surprised.' Grant, a lanky man with an impressive nose, lifted his panama to push his scanty hair back wearily and tugged the hat back into place. 'I needed that bathroom break, it's getting to me as well. Those poor lads, cut off so young. The last one was horrible. I'm glad you didn't see it.'

'Me too. Grant, you know the island really well, don't you?'

'This part of it, yes.' He gave her a surprised look. 'Not sure I'll be able to help much if you want to head to the north, for instance. But I know this region like the back of my hand.'

'And the people? Specifically Jack and Julie Rogers?'

His face closed and he looked away. 'I don't move in those circles. Lowly author, you know.' He gave an uneasy laugh and she stared into what she could see of his face.

'You hear things, though. I'll be honest with you. We're beginning to wonder what we're getting ourselves into. He isn't our sort of person either.'

'Ah.' He met her eyes again, looking relieved. 'Just whispers, you understand. Bits of gossip, here and there.'

'Such as?' She knew William was listening, and he wasn't making any move to interrupt.

'Well.' Grant glanced over to check that Jose was out of earshot. 'He's filthy rich, you know that. Something of a tyrant, doesn't like to be crossed. In recent years that has become more marked. He *really* doesn't like to be crossed. He decided he wanted to extend his land, buy up the plantation flanking his, and the owner didn't want to sell.' He looked at her worriedly. 'He was shot and killed in a street fight two weeks later. Innocent bystander. You have to understand, the islands don't have a major crime problem. People don't *get* killed, it was something of a sensation. The widow sold Rogers the land and left the island. His son Benjamin lives there now, when he's not dashing back and forth sorting out the old man's business interests. They're as bad as each other. Some funny rumours about the parties at Benjamin's place are circulating. And there's talk—okay, gossip—there's a woman the old man has taken a shine to. Lovely woman, half his age, happily married. She *was* happily married. Her husband died, too. She's still in mourning but the gossips say if they were Julie Rogers, they'd get to a safe distance. He's not a divorcing man—did it once and has complained ever since what it cost him. He won't pay out again.'

'Donald's been framed once before for the death of an inconvenient wife.' William sounded immensely tired. 'I have a very bad feeling about this.'

'Your friend Donald?' Grant looked surprised and William waved his hand dismissively.

'Thinking out loud. She and Donald have vanished. I wonder. Apparently she has a pied-à-terre where she takes her lovers, under the guise of visiting a friend. Any gossip about that?'

'Well, no, but she doesn't drive, you know. Lost her licence for good after one too many DUI charges, which even Rogers couldn't get quashed. Or maybe he even set it up, so that he'd always know where she was. So the chances are the driver knows: he'll have driven her there if you're right about her also having a love-nest.' He shrugged as they both looked surprised. 'Jack likes his actresses. It's pretty generally known he has a penthouse apartment for his adventures, and Julie ignores that. Maybe they reached an agreement a while back. She's quite discreet about her own activities, though, I'd never heard talk of any lovers. You know that limo has a built-in satnav, right? Any chance it would be listed on that?'

'Almost guaranteed, especially as Jose is new to the island. Definately got to be worth trying.' William staggered and Vivian looked alarmed and put a steadying hand on his arm. 'Good lass. I'm going to collapse. Grant, back away. As soon as the driver comes over, you can slip into the car and look.'

'What am I looking for?' Grant asked avidly and William gave him an irritated frown.

'Where's that writer imagination, man? Donald did say something about a tourist patch that was popular with Brits, and a friend called May, but any address in the sort of area that seems off the usual Rogers radar. An apartment over a shop. Be inventive.' He groaned, loudly enough to catch the driver's attention, as he glanced down. 'Bugger, that ground looks bloody hard. I'll give you as much time as I can.'

He dropped his stick, fell to his knees, then crashed sideways to the ground as Vivian shrieked piercingly and dropped into a crouch beside him. Grant backed away, then turned and ran for the car, shouting to the driver in Spanish to go help. As the startled man started forward involuntarily, Grant side-stepped and slipped behind him to reach the car.

William groaned again, and rolled away from Jose's first attempt to grip his arms. The driver, thoroughly rattled by both William's collapse and Vivian's flood of hysterics pitched at the top of her opera-trained voice, was completely caught in the sudden drama. He breathlessly appealed to William to lie still, let him check him as he was trained in first aid, then implored Vivian to translate. She deliberately misunderstood, and it was a couple of minutes before she could convince William to stop writhing. The driver checked the pulse in his neck, then started a series of questions which Vivian translated haltingly and as slowly as she dared into English.

Jose was obviously nonplussed as Vivian fed back the replies. She was tempted to struggle with the translation but didn't want him wanting Grant's fluency and looking around for him. As it was, it was only when he decided it was time to help William up that he remembered the other man and glanced across at the car, surprise becoming sudden suspicion as he saw Grant was twisted sideways in the driver's seat to look at the satnav. He scrambled from knees to his haunches to jump up and William caught his arm in one big hand.

'Help me up!'

'Ayúdame!' Vivian translated helpfully and the driver shot her a glare and tried fruitlessly to pull away. Grant glanced across, looking harassed.

'I think I have it. What the hell do we do now?'

'Time for a Scottish greeting.' William sat up convulsively, jerking hard on Jose's arm, and there was a nasty crunching sound as his forehead met the driver's nose. 'That's a Glasgow kiss, son. Have a little rest and think about it.' He retrieved his stick and got up, remarkably nimble for his size, as Grant hurried over and offered a hand, then pulled Vivian back to her feet.

'We really need a Vulcan neck pinch now, though. Whoopsie!' He hastily stepped away from Vivian, pushing her towards Grant as Jose scrambled upright, ugly with rage. Even as he rose the big driver whirled on one leg and lashed out, his foot thudding into William's well-padded side.

'You need to be a lot bigger to bring *me* down, sonny.' William grinned, sidestepped the next kick with the speed and grace that were totally at odds with his size, flicked his solid walking stick to grip it midway up the shaft, and struck a solid blow against the younger man's head.

Jose went down and stayed down, one leg twitching. William bent forward to study him thoughtfully, lips pursed. 'Better. That won't hold him long, though. Grant, help me load him in the boot of the car: we might need him again if you're wrong about the place. And you're driving. I'd crash us at the first roundabout.'

Grant started to laugh helplessly. 'Geez, I knew you were insane, but I never thought I'd get my very own William Robertson story to add to the legend. I found two possibles.' He bent to grip the driver's ankles. 'Hell, he's heavy. Solid muscle. Move the car closer?'

'I'll take one ankle.' Vivian had two spots of colour burning in her frightened cheeks, but managed a breathless laugh. 'Let's get him in before he wakes up again. William, can you manage your end?'

'Drag him over to the car by his feet. I can lift him in when we get there. Oh, and check him for a mobile phone, my lovely, we don't want him waking up and phoning ahead. What were the possibles?'

'Okay, the Patch is in Las Americas, and there *is* a May there, a Mrs May Beckett. There's also the name of a holiday resort the other way up the coast, towards my way. I can't think of any other reason why it would be in the limo satnav. Guests would surely stay with them at the finca, not in a resort. You're thinking Julie Rogers would take her lover off for a dalliance in the middle of a search?'

'No I'm not.' William bent with a grunt to heave the stirring driver into the enormous trunk of the limo with their help and brought the lid down decisively. 'But I do think that if Rogers wanted to set up some kind of lover's suicide pact, or a double murder, it makes sense to look as if they were sneaking off for a liaison. Donald mentioned that Patch place on the plane. Which one do we check first?'

'Donald knows the island,' Vivian offered. 'He'd be instantly suspicious if they didn't head straight towards Los Cristianos, and he wasn't: he phoned Kirsty from the car to say they were on their way.'

'The Patch, then. And let Kirsty know what's up. She can bring Edge up to date.' He started grinning as he got into the passenger seat beside Grant and Vivian sank gratefully into the back seat. 'I'd give a lot to see Edge buzzing grimly through the banana plantations, crouched forward over that unnatural contraption. Priceless!'

DREW

Edge was beginning to hate the Segway. Numbness was creeping up her legs from the constant slight vibration, and it was ridiculously sensitive; she only had to peer forward to look down an alternative path and it accelerated or swerved in the most unnerving fashion. Some of the tracks were in direct sun and the heat was terrific as she twisted her way down the paths. Twice the towering plantation walls ended abruptly in a dead end and she had to reverse tiredly backwards.

Her heart quickened when she saw the track she had turned into this time led to a break in the side wall, but when she reached it there was no road, just a gaping ravine. She was about to turn back when she realised a rudimentary path ran along the outside of the wall. She shuddered at the thought of riding the erratic Segway alongside a drop of several hundred feet, but for the first time she could see the main road in the distance. She drew a deep and shaky breath, then eased the transporter forward cautiously. The path widened, then bent back out of sight and she bit her lip as she crept around the corner. There was a kind of hut built against the wall and she wasn't prepared to ride around it. She would walk, and pull the Segway behind her. She got off, controlled the machine's attempt to dash forward without her, and stamped her feet gratefully on the ground. It was heavenly to be on solid ground again and she moved forward more confidently, then froze as someone shouted hoarsely from inside the hut. She was about to ride away at full speed when the shout was repeated despairingly and she caught English words.

'Help me! Please! Aidez moi! Blast it, ayúdame!'

'Drew?' Edge ran forward and rattled the padlock on the door in frustration. 'Drew, is that you? It's Edge!'

A fervent prayer was her answer and she grinned delightedly. 'We've been searching for you everywhere! But how the hell am I going to get you out?'

'I think there's a key on a nail for the padlock. I heard a clunk when they brought me water this morning. Top right, from where you are?'

'Oh wonderful, yes, a key on a string. Hang on.' She stepped gingerly onto the Segway to reach the key, but as she stepped back down it gave a fervent wriggle, twisted out of her hands and plunged down the ravine. After a moment of guilty horror at destroying a host's property, she shrugged with savage satisfaction and unlocked the padlock with shaking hands, throwing the door open as Drew, filthy, unshaven and a little wild-eyed, nearly fell into her arms.

'Bloody hell, I am so glad to see you! Is Kirsty all right? She wasn't kidnapped too?'

'She's worried sick but otherwise fine. Hang on, talk to her yourself.' Edge worked her phone free and thumbed rapidly to redial.

'Kirsty? Wonderful news, darling!' She handed the phone to Drew and moved away to peer cautiously down the ravine. The Segway hadn't, after all, bounced to the bottom but was snagged a few metres down, firmly lodged in a wedge of rock. It could, she decided, stay there. The road was barely fifty metres away now and they could surely hitch a lift the rest of the way once they reached it. Apart from the occasional car on the road there wasn't a soul in sight, but she still shushed Drew nervously when his voice went up and he quietened obediently, ended the call and handed the phone back to her.

'She says she'll phone us back in ten minutes. William and Vivian are due to call her, they're checking out a possible lead for Donald. She said you'd explain. Bloody hell.' He took in his surroundings and the ravine for the first time, and turned startled eyes on her. 'How did you get here?'

'On that.' She pointed down at the stranded machine and grinned at him. 'I would kick it if I could reach it. I'll tell you everything I know on the way down to the road. Did Kirsty think it was a good lead?'

'She said to tell you it sounded promising, and that William knocked out their driver and someone called Grant is now driving. Sounds like I had a pretty quiet time of it after all, roasting in that bloody shed.'

'You have *no* idea.' She hurried down the horrible path as quickly as she dared, talking over her shoulder as he trod at her heels, and had got to the part about stealing the Segway when they reached a tumble of boulders between them and the main road. 'Now we have to work out where the hell we are, and which way to go next.' Her phone rang and she snatched it from her pocket. 'Kirsty? Any news?'

'Still waiting to hear. William and co are on their way to Las Americas, and I'm heading that way too, I'm waiting for my taxi. Have you worked out where you are yet? Anyway, I have a car coming for you. They've got your phone on radar, so they'll be with you in ten minutes. Stay out of sight of the road and wait until a car stops and hoots twice, okay? Just to be on the safe side. May I speak to Drew again?'

He was still talking into the phone, his voice lowered, when Edge, perched on one of the handy, if uncomfortably hot, boulders, heard the two hoots and tapped him urgently on the arm. They scrambled over the big rocks onto the road, Drew quick and sure on his feet, and offering a helping hand over one tricky bit. Edge slid down rather too quickly and staggered on landing, looking about eagerly for the police car. For one horrible moment she thought they'd been tricked at the sight of the long black Mercedes, then the passenger door opened and Olga, her face as flawless and calm as ever, leaned gracefully out.

'You need a lift, I believe?'

—ele—

'At least we don't have to worry about Drew any more, but I wouldn't have thought Jack Rogers was such a fool,' William remarked as Grant cautiously rounded a smallish roundabout in the enormous limousine. He twisted his head to glance at Vivian in the back. 'When you think about it, I mean. Fools don't build financial empires. Yet he kidnaps a British citizen, which could spark an international incident in itself, drugs one of his guests, frames another to look as if he's bumped off his wife when it's already common gossip that he wants to marry again, and employs gorillas who turn nasty at the flick of a switch.' He winced theatrically and touched his side. 'It doesn't hang together.'

Vivian laughed at the wince. 'He *is* over eighty, maybe he's not as rational as he was. Grant *said* he was getting a bit extreme. And we could be creating mountains out of molehills. He's a UK citizen himself, or he was, so the kidnap could be laughed off as two Scottish nutters having a joke which went too far. Drew reappearing safe and sound, that's changed *everything*. I'm think Jack's just setting Donald and Julie up for some incriminating photographs, draped over each other in her love-nest. Having his heavy drive us off on a wild-goose chase and drugging Edge could be to keep us from interfering. If Donald and Julie are discovered covered in blushes there'll be a lot of ruffled feathers but nothing more.'

'*Serious* overkill.' William frowned at her over his shoulder and she shook her head.

'Not really, in view of the stakes. What's he worth? A *lot*, if the estate and that jet are anything to go by.'

'About fifty million euros, so rumour has it,' Grant interjected. 'Okay, allow for exaggeration, but at *least* thirty million.'

'So even if this whole exercise cost him as much as a million euros, it's a bargain. Wholesale murder would cost a lot more than that, whereas this way Julie slinks off into the sunset clutching a minimum pay-out rather than stinging him for half of everything in a divorce. It really could be as simple as that. And yes, it *is* convoluted, but Grant, you did say there are no rumours about Julie having lovers. Donald may be the only one of recent years, and it would be easy enough to prove *he's* been visiting her every year. He could have innocently upset the apple-cart by not coming in February the way he used to, and it took until now to find a way to get him here.'

William stared unseeingly at towering banana fronds visible above a retaining wall as the limousine nosed past and onto the main highway. 'Do you really think so?'

'Well, you said yourself, it's a very elaborate plot. No-one could do *that* much planning without thinking at any point, 'hang on, what if someone smells a rat?' If Julie *is* murdered, Jack has to know Donald wouldn't sit back and take the blame. And he certainly knew Donald and Edge are together. The whole trap was sprung through Drew and Kirsty to entangle Edge and therefore Donald.'

'What if he planned to murder Donald as well? Edge could be assumed to be too upset at finding he was cheating to care about investigating and he has no family, no-one else to make waves?'

'Ouch.' Vivian went quiet as she thought about it. 'That becomes seriously scary. But surely then Drew would be dead too? Once you're killing two people, a third becomes collateral damage.'

'Who is Olga?' Grant asked curiously into the pensive silence that followed. 'That was the name, right? You said someone called Olga was collecting Edge and Drew? Another Tenerife resident?'

'A neighbour of ours here on holiday with a well-connected millionaire.' Vivian's lips twitched into the involuntary grin that mention of Olga's mystery lover always provoked.

'Who might be related to Jack Rogers,' William reminded her. 'Were you already asleep on the plane when Edge said he looked like Benjamin?'

'The mystery son?' Grant was instantly interested. 'Rogers had three sons in all. Benjamin is the youngest. He was about eight years old at the time of the divorce. Jack insisted on custody—pure spite, but it was the height of the Cold War back then, and the mum was Russian, so that helped him convince the judge she was a bit dodgy. She left Scotland, moved down to London, and the oldest son, Simon, ran away when he was fourteen to join her. That was it—disowned. There was intense speculation whether he would come to his brother's funeral, as he's kept in touch with his brothers over the years, but no sign of him. That whole family is a soap opera, if you ask me.'

SIMON

'I'm Jack's son, yes.' Simon's dark eyes met Edge's in the rear view mirror. 'Don't concern yourself about it. My father and I haven't spoken in over forty years. I escaped his house as soon as I could and joined my mother in London. Her brother was a senior diplomat in the Russian embassy. We were under his protection, so there was nothing my father could do to get me back, although it was ugly for a while. He never forgave me.'

Edge, who had been gratefully wiping her grimy face and hands with scented wipes which Olga had wordlessly offered, still felt a little awkward. 'I don't know how much Kirsty told Olga of what your father has been up to?'

'Everything, I believe. I can only think he must be senile. I make it a point of keeping tabs on my relatives, so I did know there is a woman he would *like* to marry, a younger woman, in her early forties. An old man's fancy. He would soon enough realize a woman of that age, with young children and who may yet want more children, wouldn't be the ideal wife. But then who knows? Jim was his favourite son. He may want more children, to make up for the disappointments of me and Benjamin. He is not a *good* man, but there is a big difference between selfish and murderous. I think we'll find it is a simple case of incriminating photographs, so that if this young widow is open to his advances, he has a weapon against Julie for the divorce.'

A smile glimmered faintly.

'Some of your suspicions are definitely wrong. You thought he was drugging young women at parties at the estate, but there are *never* parties at the finca. He keeps a penthouse apartment in Los Cristianos for his occasional liaisons. The most entertaining he and Julie do at home is with houseguests.'

He glanced at her again in the mirror.

'My brother, on the other hand, *does* have parties. He's got into trouble more than once and my father has paid, and pulled strings, to make the trouble go away. Drugs, and some unsavoury incidents with unsuspecting tourists. Some months ago I met a woman at an event in London who thought I was Benjamin, and nearly attacked me. When she had calmed down, she told me her Tenerife experience. It was a shock. Benjamin and I are not close—I always got on better with Jim—but I wouldn't have expected that of him.'

The huge Mercedes changed lanes and he slowed to take a complicated route through intersecting roads as they left the motorway.

'She tried to investigate on her own, so far as she could. She asked the barman of her hotel if he had ever seen the man she had been drinking with. He didn't know the man, but he did tell her he had been asked more than once about women who had gone to parties with various men, because of odd incidents. I was interested enough to arrange with the Guardia Civil that I be notified of any new complaints. Unfortunately that has had, sometimes, the opposite effect. For every officer who will notify me, there is another officer who will stubbornly suppress and even reject the entire case, maybe because of my father, maybe only because I interfered. It would have been better, perhaps, if I had let the law take its own course. The cases where I was informed, I had tests done at my own laboratories but nothing was ever found. You may not know that different tests have to be used for different drugs. There is one combination I once knew of, which was hormone based, and we *have* found elevated hormonal levels but nothing conclusive. Whatever was used doesn't linger in the system.'

'The woman we saw must have been one of the suppressed cases,' Edge nodded. 'She was *furious*. Of course, your brother's finca would now be part of the whole estate, which explains why she was saying Casa Foca. That never occurred to me. So you're saying Donald and Julie will reappear, along with some fairly disastrous photographs, and that will be that?'

'I believe so. Unfortunately the photographs will have already been taken: we are nearly three hours behind events. Unlikely we will even catch the photographer, he will be long gone.'

'And you know where Julie's apartment is?'

'We are perhaps ten minutes away, depending on traffic. I think your friends will already be there. They were on their way when we last spoke to Kirsty. She will be waiting downstairs for us by the time we get there. I told you, the Rogers family keep tabs on each other.'

The big car started down towards Las Americas and she glanced distractedly out of the tinted windows as the road widened and became an avenue with ornamental trees down the centre. He commented briefly to Olga in Russian and she nodded, found a roll of peppermints and gave him one before offering them over the back of the seat. Edge was briefly diverted—of course, it must have been his uncle in the Russian embassy who helped Olga, and introduced them. Could they have been together such a long time, though? That would set something of a world record for long-term affairs. She didn't entirely care for him herself: he was a little too reasonable about her panicky suspicions, even slightly amused. If it was purely a sleazy set-up, Drew's kidnapping had brought Donald to the island at the expense of Kirsty's extreme distress, and that was unforgivable. And her drugging this morning . . . although, if Simon was right, it was probably Benjamin who had drugged her coffee. On Jack's orders? He had certainly known about it, his smirk when she nearly passed out in front of him had proved that.

It did seem odd, though, that Benjamin would connive at his father divorcing Julie to be able to marry again, especially to marry a woman young enough to have more children. That would surely be the very last thing that a son who worked so hard to stay in favour with a difficult father would want?

She frowned, blocking out a question Olga was politely asking Drew about his incarceration. It *was* the last thing Benjamin would want. He was subservient to his father, but there had been that flash of contempt in that glance he shot his father this morning. A theory was taking shape in her mind that she didn't like at all, but if one son was trying to secure his inheritance, was the other totally to be trusted? In which case she was in the worst possible company to be attempting a rescue. Speak up? Keep her mouth shut and hope she was wrong? She found herself fervently wishing William was in the car, because he was so very good at theories and might also be able to convince so-smooth Simon to drive a little faster . . .

RESCUED

'Where now?' William bent forward to peer out of the window as the limousine eased around a roundabout and Grant shrugged helplessly.

'The satnav says we're within a hundred yards. I'm trying to find parking but that's close to impossible in this area. Keep your eyes peeled.'

'There are *hundreds* of apartments!' Vivian was staring out the back window in dismay. 'Is there no address at all?'

'Nope. Okay, this is it. And not a parking spot in sight. Let me drop you off here at this café. I'll go find somewhere to park. If you're not at the café I'll wait there until you phone and tell me where you are.'

William got out nimbly with the aid of his stick and helped Vivian out of the back in the impatient traffic. They stepped clear of the road onto the pavement, hands still clasped, and William tilted his head back to scan the holiday apartments rising two and three storeys along either side of the road as the big car slid away. 'Okay, that big place is a hotel, so at least that's out. But where do we start?'

'Do we even need to? Let's face it, Donald will be embarrassed enough to be caught in the nuddie with his lady love without us gawping at him into the bargain.' Vivian sounded deflated and William squeezed her hand reprovingly.

'Would you stop Edge rescuing me from a humiliating moment, if the tables were turned?'

'Edge would need to rescue you *from* me, if the tables were turned. I don't feel—William, that's Benjamin Rogers! Walking quickly, there, look. I'm *sure!*'

'Could be. I just got a glimpse before he went in that apartment block. Follow him? If he's in on the thing that would *really* embarrass Donald. Adding us into the equation would hardly register.'

'Yes, follow him. He looked a man on a mission. Hurry!'

Benjamin was cutting across the reception area of the apartment block, which opened ahead into the shared garden, heading confidently for the stairs. Vivian started up after him as he rounded the first landing, leaving William, who wasn't very swift on stairs, to haul himself up in her wake. The staircase door slammed above and she opened it moments later to peer cautiously through the crack. He was waiting impatiently three doors along the open corridor, leaning over the waist-high wall to glare down at the swimming pool in the central garden, but even as she flinched back the apartment door must have opened, because he whirled and started talking in angry Spanish. As William puffed up to join her, Benjamin strode through the apartment door and it slammed shut.

'Well?' William panted impatiently and she pulled the staircase door open, lowering her voice.

'Third door along, and I think we're in time! He was asking how the hell they could let him barricade himself in the bathroom!'

William laughed breathlessly and punched the air. 'Superb! To the rescue, then! Phone Grant and tell him which building and the apartment number first so he can call the police. *Not* good if Benjamin and his henchman turn ugly.'

Vivian tiptoed along the passage to check the apartment number and phoned Grant while William got his breathing back under control. He heaved a final deep breath, took a firm grip of his stick, and strode down to the door. He glanced at her for her nod as she ended the call, and rapped smartly with the head of the stick. No response. He hammered more loudly, then raised his stentorian voice.

'I'm going to carry on making a noise, Rogers. You might as well open up.'

There was a startled interchange on the far side of the door before it opened. Benjamin, flushed and annoyed, glared up at the bigger man.

'What the hell? This is a private apartment, I'm visiting a friend!'

'Me too.' William beamed down at him. 'Donald invited us along. This is your stepmother's apartment, right? We have the right address?'

Benjamin stared at him. 'What? Did Jose bring you? Where is he?'

'Parking the car. Donald phoned us, told us where to come.'

Benjamin frowned, then stepped back sullenly and opened the door wide. 'Come in, then.' He closed the door behind them and flicked the lock across as William and Vivian moved past him. Two heavily-built men were standing impassively next to what was presumably the barricaded bathroom door. The room was dimly lit with the curtains drawn against the sun, small, and simply furnished. Apart from a boudoir couch, the bulk of the space was taken up by a large bed where Julie Rogers, her hair spread across the pillow and a sheet thrown over her, lay sleeping.

'There has been, unfortunately, a terrible accident,' Benjamin said throatily, and his mirthless smile appeared as Vivian glanced at him, surprised. 'Or perhaps I should say, there is about to be a terrible accident.'

She gave an involuntary snort of nervous laughter at his melodramatic manner, then blinked as he drew a handgun from his pocket and pointed it at them, stepping back out of range of William's stick.

'An orgy. My slut of a stepmother invited her lover and his friends to partake in some adulterous fun but alas, they got carried away. Take off your clothes, please. All your clothes. You are about to enjoy some very classy drugs. Sadly, I believe you will overdose. Very sad indeed.'

It was so incredibly corny that she felt another half-hysterical giggle bubbling up. Impossible to take him seriously—but impossible not to be alarmed by the automatic. A fool can fire a gun as surely as an assassin, and with as much devastating effect, but he was so ludicrous that she shook with disastrous laughter and leaned back weakly against the front door. He shot her a suspicious look, but took her tortured expression as terror and looked back at William.

'Nothing happens until you get that bathroom door opened.' William glanced calmly at the gun, and raised his voice. 'Donald? You okay, mate?'

'Oh aye, but no window, I cannae get out,' Donald shouted back from the bathroom. William nodded and looked Benjamin steadily in the eye.

'Not going to work, pal. We're not taking off our clothes. If you shoot us, you have bullet holes to explain away, not to mention a lot of noise. There's a fair number of people sitting round that pool downstairs, and sound carries.' He leaned on his stick, suddenly looking exhausted. 'If you try to undress us by force, trust me, there will be even more noise. Not to mention that my friend is calling the police right now.'

Benjamin nodded, still smiling. 'No matter, although it gets messier. This lady here followed her lover in a jealous fury. He hero-ically barricades himself in the bathroom, while she shoots Julie as she sleeps. Or you burst down the bathroom door – you are big enough for that to be credible—and shoot him. Shoot everyone, then yourself. The police here know all British tourists are insane; who shot who will hardly interest them.'

His eyes had a fixed triumphant stare which looked worryingly far from rational and Vivian shuddered and snorted again, still leaning against the door. He gestured at her with the gun, and William lurched forward clumsily, leaning heavily on his stick. Benjamin stepped back smartly, not buying it, and the tension in the room jumped.

For a moment all attention was on them and Vivian reached behind her to flick the locking mechanism back to open, stepping forward to block the door with her body as she did, her half-hysterical laughter gone as quickly as it had surged. No chance of making a dash for it without precipitating a crisis, but at least now Grant could walk in. That might be enough of a distraction for William to do something. What he could hope to do against three strong and hostile men un-less he could get the gun, she couldn't begin to imagine. But he was William. Sixty if he was a day, overweight, big enough to look clumsy, but quicker and stronger than anyone ever expected.

She moved into the room obediently as Benjamin looked across again to jerk his head at her. The two Spaniards resumed their assault on the bathroom door, which grudgingly opened a crack. One of the men gave a breathless grunt of satisfaction and pushed with renewed vigour and the door opened a little more.

They were all staring, fascinated, when the front door opened, but it wasn't Grant. For a puzzled moment Vivian thought Benjamin was in two places at once, and then she realized this man was older, a little broader. The brother.

'Benjamin.' Simon filled the doorway as the brothers stared at each other, then Simon glanced around the room, taking in the situation instantly. 'You *want* our father free to marry again, have more children?'

'*No!*' Benjamin looked exasperated. 'He wants rid of Julie. I told him about her long-term affair, suggested the photographs, and how to get her lover here. He liked it. *He* set it up.'

'And you're changing the plan.' Simon ambled in to perch calmly on the edge of the bed and his brother relaxed fractionally. 'You always were quick as a whip,' he said grudgingly. 'It was easy to change. She dies, the lover dies, the old man is found to have made all the arrangements, he gets charged with murder. The shock kills him. The entire estate comes to me. To us, I should say. If you want half. You do have plenty of your own.'

Simon raised his eyebrows and Benjamin shrugged. 'If he divorces her, marries this other woman, she will fall pregnant whatever way she can—his child or another's—and claim everything I have worked for so hard all these years. I would share with *you*, I would be happy to, but not with a changeling. What else could I do?'

Simon studied him curiously, then gave a slight nod in response. 'How do you know he won't tell the police your part in the plan? He's a tough old bugger. You can't be sure the shock will kill him.'

'Yes, I can.' Benjamin eyed him cautiously and Simon nodded again, utterly unruffled.

'Not just recreational drugs, then.'

'I don't do drugs at all. My guests sometimes do. While I was working out how to use the old man's formula to best effect, trying a tweak here and there to make it more interesting, there was an accident. Turns out with one added chemical the old wasp was pretty lethal.'

'And still untraceable?' Simon looked interested. 'I did wonder once or twice whether you'd got his secret formula from him all those years ago.' He glanced mildly at William. 'My father made, um, art films a long time back. The sex drug of choice back then was Spanish Fly. He developed an alternative. It amused him to call it Scottish Wasp. Just a pinch, and his actors and actresses were *much* more interested in the script.'

He seemed to lose interest in the conversation and looked back at his brother. 'I hate the old man, you know that, and I despise and loathe Julie for the damage she caused. I'm not going to stop you. And I'm not interested in the money.'

Benjamin half-laughed and for the first time lowered the gun. 'Easy to say when you marry an heiress. How is my beautiful sister-in-law?'

'The same. She never complains. She sends me away on my holidays with a smile on her face and no bitterness in her heart.' He flicked a hand dismissively. 'I won't stop you, but do the others have to die? It will cause a much bigger investigation, apart from anything else.'

Benjamin lifted his shoulder helplessly. 'The police are already on their way, we have to move fast. I only ever intended Julie and her lover to die and she *deserved* it, cheating on the old man all these years. Her lover deserves it too, the filthy adulterer. The others forced themselves in, changed everything.'

Simon shook his head. 'I stopped the police. That's sorted. I have nearly as much pull as the old man when it comes to that. Seems to me, though—'

The bathroom door finally gave way at that point with a screech as the marble vanity stand slid away, and the bigger of the two men pushed through. Sounds of an urgent scuffle reached the others, and the second man looked startled, then followed.

Simon raised his voice slightly over the breathless cursing and gasps. 'Seems to *me* we should keep the noise down before someone else calls them, eh?'

Benjamin barked out an order and the noise in the bathroom abruptly stopped. There was a momentary pause before Donald was pushed into the main room, still naked, looking very dishevelled and with one eye rapidly closing. Simon glanced contemptuously at him, leaned forward to pick up the shirt draped on the end of the bed, and tossed it to him.

'Cover yourself. Disgusting.'

Donald tied the shirt sheepishly around his midriff as Vivian shot William a quick questioning glance. He was frowning slightly, watching Simon closely, but seemed to feel her glance and looked up briefly, flicking one eye in a half-wink. So he wasn't buying it. She drew what felt like her first deep breath since they had entered the apartment. True enough, Simon might have done something unpleasant to Edge and Drew, but surely not to Olga? And Olga would *never* connive at murder.

It was as though Benjamin had picked Olga from her thoughts, and his heavy brows drew together. 'Where is your woman? I had word you'd arrived a few days ago with her—oh, yes, I have my own sources. I didn't expect to see you *here*. What brought you, anyway? How did you *know*?'

Simon shrugged dismissively. 'She is friends with these people. That's the reason I ask for their lives. I can even help there. You know, one useful side-effect of the Wasp was that it sometimes caused short-term memory loss, right? I was intrigued by that. I stole a vial of it before I ran away. A few years ago I arranged for some very skilled experimenting.'

He grinned tightly at his brother.

'We are very alike, you and I, Ben, and you know my resources. I got that side perfected. There's a crashing headache, twelve hours of deep sleep and – no memory of the last twenty-four hours. We could get them away, give them my version of the Wasp, and you're back to your original plan. Clean and tidy.'

Expressions were following each other on Benjamin's face—interest, suspicion, disbelief.

'Check the passageway,' he said in Spanish to one of his men, and shot his thin smile at his brother. 'Not that I don't trust you, bro. But you still haven't explained how you came to be *here*.'

'Ben.' Simon smiled and shook his head. The Spaniard leaned out the open doorway and froze for several seconds, then turned back, his face suddenly sallow.

'Nada.' It couldn't have been less convincing, but even as Benjamin tensed and lifted the gun Simon made a lunge for it. He nearly made it, his fingertips brushing the metal as Benjamin stepped swiftly backwards out of range, his face twisting with rage . . . but he stepped in the wrong direction. William's arms clamped around him like a vice and Simon reached forward and carefully took the gun from his brother's trapped hand.

'Thank you.' He nodded to William. 'He was quicker than I expected. Luckily, so were you.' He raised his voice. 'You can come in. We'll get nothing more. Damn,' he added in almost an undertone as five officers in the distinctive green Guardia Civil uniforms, looking stern, filed into the room, swiftly and efficiently cuffing the three men and moving them out. The senior officer and Simon spoke briefly in Spanish too quick for anyone but Donald to follow, then left the room. Vivian averted her eyes politely as Donald raised his brows and sat down on the bed, reaching for his clothes to quickly dress.

'What was that about?' William asked curiously. 'And quality shiner, mate. You okay?'

'I'll live. Simon had them listening in to get what they could on the drug front, I gather. Nobody's thrilled.'

'No, we're not.' Simon re-entered the room as Donald spoke. 'You decent yet? Okay, ladies, come on in.'

REUNITED

Olga and Edge entered cautiously, Edge looking horrified when she saw Donald's battered face. She glanced once at Julie, still deeply asleep, and crouched down in front of him to run gentle fingers over his eye. He winced and shifted his head away, catching at her hand to kiss it briefly, and she smiled at him.

'You'll live. Not as handsome as you were, but an icepack or two should sort that.'

'I want a steak.' He took her face between his hands and kissed her gratefully. 'A giant one. Cooked, though. I just hope the polis can get Drew's location out of Benjamin so I can get one soon. I'm bloody starving.'

Her face lit with laughter. 'Oh, I already found Drew.' She flipped a nonchalant hand. 'Kirsty met us downstairs and they went off in the car to find parking. Olga and I felt we would be surplus to requirements, so we crept upstairs to listen. My poor love, I didn't realize you'd been beaten up.'

'Better than dead,' he said drily and looked across at Simon. 'You're a bloody good actor, mate, had me quaking in my boots. If I had had boots. What was that about the drugs?'

Simon sighed. 'My disastrous little brother got hold of a fairly innocent formula my father used to use to make his actors less inhibited, and re-jigged it. He's been making a bit of a beast of himself ever since with female tourists, and I'm also pretty sure he was behind Jim's death. I'll never believe Jim went to sleep behind the wheel of his car: he was a careful driver. Trouble is, without knowing the formula, it's been impossible to get a usable test for it. I was trying to lead him along to the point where we could discuss ingredients, but he was a little too paranoid.'

William was surprised into a laugh. 'So you were bluffing about stealing a vial of it? Donald's right, you *are* good.' He sat down on the boudoir couch with a sigh of relief and glanced up at Vivian, patting the remaining space invitingly.

'Would a sample help?' Edge straightened up from her crouching position. 'I don't know if it's the same drug, of course, but he put *something* into my coffee this morning. I poured at least half a cupful into a sort of urn thing next to my chair on the patio. It should still be there.'

'Ah!' Simon leaned forward, grasped her shoulders in strong hands, and planted firm kisses either side of her mouth. 'Mrs Cameron, thank you very much. That was very clever of you. If it is the drug, you will have to stay in Tenerife to give evidence, but don't worry, not at Casa Foca. You can stay at the villa I am renting. All of you. Okay?'

'Um, okay,' she said uncertainly and he grinned at her, suddenly strikingly attractive. He released her to turn to Olga with a quick sentence in Russian, then strode from the room after the police.

'Wow.' She looked across at Olga. 'What a transformation! Is he always like that?'

'Not alvays.' Olga smiled, looking impish. 'Not many see that side of him, you have made him very happy. That makes me happy. It vill be good to have you with us at the villa. You can fly back vith us, too.'

'It just occurred to me,' William interjected from across the room, 'that if we can time this right, we've got the perfect excuse to miss Fiona and Brian's wedding. We'll be helping the Guardia Civil of Tenerife with their enquiries.' He beamed beatifically and leaned back comfortably. 'Ouch. I've got a massive bruise coming up where that bloody driver kicked me. That's probably evidence, too. I wonder if the polis have rescued him from the trunk of the limousine yet?'

Julie grunted suddenly, rolled onto her back and opened her eyes, blinked in horror and clutched the sheet up to her chin as she realized she was in her secret apartment, and it was full of people.

—ele—

'It wasn't the time, and it wasn't the place.' Drew looked ruefully at Edge as Kirsty leaned across the café table to show Vivian her ring. 'I just blurted it out. Thank God she went for it.'

After a brief and somewhat difficult explanation, mainly from William, Julie had ordered them out of the apartment so she could dress and they had trooped thankfully downstairs to the street to join Grant, Drew and Kirsty at the big café, pulling two of its tables together into the deepest shade. Even in the shade the afternoon heat was stifling and their sangria glasses were sweating with condensation.

Their party drew a couple of curious glances—Edge was still bedraggled after her ride through the plantations, Donald's eye had swollen shut and bulged above and below his shades, and Drew looked thoroughly dishevelled. William had suggested they sit at a separate table, and complained that his reputation on the island was now lost beyond redemption. Grant told him his reputation had preceded him and there was nothing to lose anyway. They were all a little hilarious with reaction, and reluctant to move on.

'You'll never look worse than you do right now,' Donald told Drew, gingerly pushing his shades back up his battered nose. 'At least you know she *has* to be potty about you to have said yes. You heading back to your flash apartment for a shower anytime, or planning to stay with the butch unshaven and unwashed look for a while? It doesnae suit you.'

Edge snorted with laughter. 'It just occurred to me, that flash apartment is probably Jack's love-nest, in which case he'll be wanting it back. Julie didn't seem at all impressed with his nasty little plan, so he's going to need a bolt-hole. Maybe we should go back with them, Donald, and have a look before they're evicted? I've never seen a millionaire's seduction pad before.'

'We're effectively evicted too,' he reminded her. 'One way and another, I don't think pitching up at Casa Foca is going to be an option. Julie won't want us cramping her style. She's got a fair pair of lungs on her and we don't want to be anywhere in the vicinity when she starts in on Jack. It won't be remotely relaxing. I wonder if we can claim insurance on our luggage if we say we were too scared to collect it?'

Olga laughed. 'The servants vill pack it up and bring it to the place Simon is renting, don't vorry about that. And you vill love the villa.'

'Is it a banana plantation?' Edge asked suspiciously and Olga shook her head. She sighed with relief. 'I like it already. I don't think I'll ever look at a banana again without wincing.'

Donald grinned and rose to his feet a little stiffly to get them more drinks. Everyone else was talking at once, but the two women sat for a moment in comfortable silence. Olga sighed and looked at Edge a little ruefully.

'*Yes*, he's married. Natalia vas my first friend in London. Simon's uncle introduced us and ve became best friends. I vas chief bridesmaid ven she married Simon. Less than a year later she had a fall out hunting, broke her neck. Never any question of divorce, and he and her family never stopped searching for a treatment. They invested heavily in medical research, and he still does. It has made him very rich but he vould give it all up in a heartbeat to have her as she vas. She vill not let me visit her, but she insists he takes holidays every year, and that the holidays be vith me because she trusts me.' She met Edge's eyes squarely. 'She knows, but she also knows I vill never demand he divorce her, never make us all unhappy. Despite everything, it is a good marriage. He is a good man.'

Edge squeezed her hand in silent empathy. 'That was the turning point for me, when I was panicking in the car about speaking up about Benjamin. I *knew* you couldn't care for a man who could be involved in anything like this. I knew he had to be a good guy.'

Donald returned with another two jugs of sangria, and a rose, which he put next to Edge's glass.

'And this?' She was surprised and unexpectedly touched.

He winced slightly as he sat down. 'I dreamed about you calling me, you know. It woke me. When I realized where I was, even before I knew what was actually going on, terror of what you'd do dragged me fully awake.' He shot her a sly grin, then turned serious. 'I might be dead by now if you had believed their plan—that I was cheating on you. When I was in that bathroom, braced against that bloody vanity with my feet against the bath, trying to hold the door shut, all I could think was that I had to stay alive, to explain to you. It was the most important thing in the world. So I'm courting you. A little bit. For as long as you like it, anyway.'

Edge laughed. 'What's involved in courting?'

'A bubble-bath by candlelight.' He topped up her glass. 'A walk along a moonlit beach. Roses for no reason. Hell, I don't know, I'll have to ask Drew or look it up on the internet, I've never done anything like this myself. I do know that I didn't realize how much you meant to me until I thought I was going to lose you. I'm incredibly glad you turned out to be a woman in more than a billion.' She gave him a puzzled look and he shook his head at her. 'Don't you remember?'

'Yes, I said I *wasn't* a woman in a billion, that I'd come hot-footing after you if you disappeared with Julie. And I did.'

'Believing the worst. You must have done. A woman in a mere million who learned an hour or two down the line that her man had popped off with his ex would have been enraged. You still trusted me. I'm here, I'm alive, because you did. I want a minute-by-minute breakdown of that ride through the plantations while I was snoring my head off.'

'We're all going to be exchanging stories.' William, who had phenomenally good hearing and was unabashedly eavesdropping, grinned at them. 'I'm too modest to tell you my bit, but I was magnificent. Vivian can tell you, while I describe her flitting up the stairs behind Benjamin like Nemesis. It's been one helluva day.'

'And is definitely siesta time,' Grant said regretfully and swayed slightly as he pushed himself to his feet. 'I hope I don't fall asleep in the taxi, after all this sangria. William, it's been great to see you again. Mucho gusto to the rest of you, and I wish *you* two.' to Kirsty and Drew, 'a long and happy life together, and no more excitement. The rest of this holiday will be quite an anti-climax for you.'

AFTERMATH

Drew pointed out to his employers that a chance to watch another country's legal process swing into action was too good to miss, and Police Scotland also decided it could be a positive advantage to maintain good relations between the police forces of the two countries by loaning them a sergeant temporarily. They were therefore able to enjoy not only their last few days in the penthouse but to join the villa party. He has decided not to pursue the matter of his kidnapping, since it came with so many advantages. He says he will, however, be very cautious about the next travel offer that looks too good to be true. Kirsty's opinion of the Guardia Civil has soared, and she has started Spanish lessons.

Jack tried to pull in every favour he could command, but only on his own behalf: he no longer has the slightest interest in fathering more sons. It seems likely that Julie, after coolly weighing up all her options, will once again choose in his favour. Edge has privately decided that is sufficient punishment.

———ℓℓ———

One mooted date for the start of the formal trial is indeed the day of Fiona and Brian's wedding, much to Edge and Vivian's relief, and they have sent their regrets and best wishes to the happy couple. William is facing the prospect of more flights with equanimity, since the main witness needed at the same time is generous with his private plane.

———ℓℓ———

However, they have decided to remain in Tenerife for the few weeks until the initial hearing. Edge's cat, Mortimer, has settled happily enough with her aunt, and Odette and Buster, in the house kennels, aren't pining as the Major is happy to continue walking them twice a day on the condition, he says, that he gets the first scoop on their adventures.

———ℓℓ———

The official results of the tests on the so-called Scottish Wasp are being held secret pending the trial but private tests done on a retained sample of Jim's blood confirmed his murder. Now that the formula is known, and could be traced in the other blood samples, generous compensation will be offered to the known rape victims and should pay for their holidays for the rest of their lives. They may or may not, in view of their experiences, decide to take those holidays in Tenerife.

—⁓⁓—

For those who are interested in such things, it was invented for the story but if it had existed would have included hormones already naturally occurring in the human body—specifically testosterone and LH (luteinising hormone) which both affect sex drive, progesterone, for its feel-good factor, and melatonin, the sleep hormone. Jack's original Wasp would have made his actors and actresses extremely sensual. His son found that adding a relatively small amount of chloral hydrate (the original Mickey Finn knockout drug) resulted in a deep but receptive sleep. Any tests done a few hours later specifically for chloral hydrate would have found it in such small quantities as to be inconclusive, while the hormones would, within a few hours, be showing as high but no longer abnormal. The combination certainly made Edge far bolder than she would normally have been, brave enough to climb down from the balcony and steal the Segway despite the chloral hydrate in her system. When he instead added a popular recreational drug, again in small quantities, the compound punch was fatal for the unfortunate tourist. It looks at this point as though he will be charged primarily with the murder at of his brother, rather than the tourist's accidental death, the shooting of the original owner of the neighbouring plantation, or the attempted murders.

Despite the above explanation I suspect I have torpedoed my chances of ever being admitted to the Detection Club, circa 1929, as it is strict on the subject of untraceable drugs and poisons. Tchah. However it is not strictly true to the pure whodunit anyway, with some clues given to the reader which weren't known to the sleuths.

—ele—

This is, as will be obvious, a work of purest fiction and I hope the various police forces of Tenerife, who do a superb job of keeping the island peaceful and remarkably crime-free, will forgive any implications against individuals who do not, after all, exist. Liberties, both accidental and deliberate, have been taken with geography and although the towns named, and even the Patch, do exist, the specific apartments in the story are invented. So, of course, is Case Foca, which got its name purely to sound like a word which would catch the attention of someone who spoke no Spanish. Tenerife itself is much as described—stark and beautiful in equal parts.

—ele—

Segways do make your legs go numb within half an hour, but I personally found them far more fun to ride than Edge did. On the other hand, I was tootling round the boulevards and side streets of Las Americas rather than steaming alongside banana plantations. That probably helped.

—ele—

An excerpt follows for *Fifteen Sixteen Maids In The Kitchen*, which is possibly my favourite in the series - it is certainly the most conventional, a whodunit in a manor house with a house-party, complete (of course) with a body in the library.

If you enjoyed this story, I'd be deeply grateful if you'd add a review, because my readers are flagging by this stage of the series, and can't face putting up yet another. If you could only consider, as I do, the reader looking for stories about Tenerife and this is the first in the series they stumble across, you'd see how I can still be looking hopeful? I know. It's an imposition. But –

GLOSSARY

Bidey-in – live-in partner

Bottled it – lost his nerve (not only Scottish)

Blether – chat, gossip

Burled – turned quickly

De nada – it is nothing (Spanish)

Dinna fash (also dinnae fash) – don't worry

Finca – country house (Spanish)

Footie – football (soccer)

Ken – know, to know

Lo siento – I am sorry (Spanish)

No hablo Inglés – I don't speak English

Mucho gusto – pleased to meet you (Spanish)

Numpty – idiot.

Swithered – unable to decide

Tanatorio – funeral parlour (Spanish)

OTHER BOOKS YOU MAY ENJOY

NINETEEN TWENTY MY PLATE IS EMPTY
THE CHRISTMAS CAPER (novella)
ONE TO SIX (box-set)

Also by EJ Lamprey
DO-OVER (thriller)
THE PASSING OF MRS PARKER WOODBURN (novella)
PIDGIN SPANISH (non-fiction)
Children's novella
THE KIDNAP CAPER

Writing as Joanna Lamprey
NO PLACE LIKE PLACE – The Talian Project (book 1)
NO PLACE LIKE PLACE – The Missionaries (book 2)
TIME AFTER TIME (short stories and novella)

Writing as Clarissa Rodgers-Briskleigh
A SECOND RAINBOW
THE MONEY HONEY
Non-fiction
ON PERFECTING YOUR INDIAN SUMMER
LOOKING FOR MR WILL-DO-NICELY

ACKNOWLEDGMENTS AND THANKS

Artwork by Lacey O'Connor
Manuscript review by Stephanie Dagg

Thanks also to "Alex" who answered reams of questions and drove me round Adeje and the coastal towns on several successive visits. It is partly due to his introduction to life in Spanish islands that I live now in Spain itself.

And of course as always, thanks to my beta readers, for their intelligent questions and sharp eyes, and particularly Barbara, Andrew, Charlie, Helen and Susan, my valued regulars, from all round the world: Scotland, South Africa, the US and Canada. Anyone who uses quality beta readers knows what impact they have on the final product. 'Thanks' doesn't begin to cover it.

About the author

Elizabeth (EJ) Lamprey moved to the Costa Tropical area of Granada, Spain, in 2017. Originally from South Africa, she's the daughter of a Scot, looks like a Scot, dearly loved Scotland, but after fifteen years of Scottish winters couldn't resist a return to a life in the sun. She has been variously a book reviewer on a city paper, a columnist in a national magazine, a copy-editor and book critic, a commercial blogger, and a reporter on a country newspaper, earning an actual living with more conventional jobs.

She shares her Spanish guest house with her rescued podenco and an intermittent series of eccentric (or even, occasionally, conventional) guests, teaches English as a second language online, still hasn't improved much past pidgin Spanish, writes as often as she can, is besotted with her new granddaughter, and loves being a part-time *jubilada*.

FIFTEEN SIXTEEN MAIDS IN THE KITCHEN

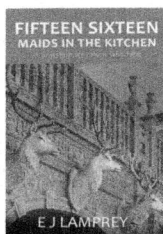

EXCERPT

'Couldn't do this without four wheel drive, at a guess.' Donald Mc-Donald, sitting in the back seat, leaned forward to peer through the windscreen as William Robertson hastily reached for the knob on the dashboard to engage terrain response and his big Range Rover clambered slowly through the short tunnel under the railway line. The track was so neglected it had eroded into a gully, and the rain, which had been falling most of the night, had turned it into a waterway. The Range Rover groaned, wheels spinning, then took hold and they were through with a lurch that jolted Vivian Oliver's handbag off her lap into the footwell of the passenger seat. 'What did your uncle drive, a tractor? Or is there another access?'

'No other access, and no-one else lives here, so he just organized a couple of tons of gravel put down every autumn to keep it accessible over winter. It's not usually this bad, but then we've had a crappy summer.'

'He was the only one living in the glen? At *ninety?*' Edge Cameron, sitting with Donald in the back seat, was startled. They emerged into a rolling landscape which stretched as far as the eye could see, bright gorse against rough grass and occasional trees against the slopes of the surrounding hills. 'Wow, did you inherit all *this?*'

'Yes and no.' William glanced at her slightly impatiently in the rear-view mirror. 'The whole glen, bar the lodge itself, was sold on a hundred-year lease to a big syndicate. Their guys come in by tractor, so they don't care what the road is like. There's a team of cleaners that come through every month; not for the last two months, of course. They seemed to manage. More gravel would sort the problem short-term but that's another thing the Foundation wants properly fixed before they'll consider taking the place off my hands. Imagine what *that* would cost?'

The rain stopped, and the clouds parted to finally allow a few thin rays of late morning sunshine.

'Deer!' Edge pointed, delighted, and Vivian's labrador Buster barked sharply from the back. Donald's whippet reared on her dainty hind legs to sniff urgently at his opened window over his shoulder.

'Aye, the syndicate farms free range red deer. Always been deer here, hence the shooting lodge. With *serious* delusions of grandeur.' He turned off the track to rattle across an enormous cattle grid onto a weed-choked gravel driveway between banks of overgrown towering hedges, which widened to reveal a parking area around a dilapidated fountain.

'That's it, we're here.' He brought the Range Rover to a crunching halt and twisted round to look at Edge and Donald. 'What do you think?'

Donald craned his neck again to look through the front windscreen. 'That's big. That's *extremely* big.'

Edge opened her door to get out of the car and shaded her eyes against the watery sun to look up. 'Heavens, William, it's *very* baronial. When you said a shooting lodge, I pictured a cabin in the woods! And you never answered my earlier question, did he live here alone?'

'Pretty much. For a while he had a male carer living in to cook and take care of him. That ended when Butler, the land agent, noticed the carer was helping himself to things, so he had to go. For the last few years the old man was paying way over the odds to have carers coming in morning and evening instead, and fiercely resisting being moved out. He solved the problem by dying peacefully in his bed, exactly the way he wanted to go. And aye, it's huge. Ten bedrooms, four reception rooms. Only three bathrooms, but you could hold a party in each.' He grinned at them, a sudden easing of his bad mood of recent weeks. 'Has to be seen to be believed. Vivian nearly passed out when she saw the kitchen.'

'Neither Edge nor I are kitchen experts.' Donald creased his vivid blue eyes as he got out of the car to stare up at the sprawling mansion. 'Not yet seeing why you asked us to join you. Are you thinking of doing it up, or just letting it collapse into a picturesque ruin?'

'It's a complete drain on my finances, and will get worse. I was thinking of hosting at least one murder weekend, though, as a bit of a fund-raiser. Wait until you see inside. My uncle was an illusionist, a good one, who became a special effects expert. He even spent a couple of years in Hollywood, before the computer graphics revolution ended the demand for his services in the late seventies. He did horror, mainly, and this house includes every optical and mechanical effect he ever thought up. He never quite forgave his peers for refusing to recognize his contributions to prestidigitation because of the film side. This was his way of giving them the finger and preserving his genius. It's pure *nasty*. I thought, hmm, who do I know who understands set design, who could draw out the final ounce of drama? Or for that matter, who could script a suitable plot? I couldn't think of anyone.' He looked slyly at them, and Edge laughed aloud.

'I'm a sitcom scriptwriter,' she protested. 'I've never written a murder plot in my life! But actually that's an inspired idea. All this place needs is a couple of ravens croaking from the roof, it *shrieks* dark deeds. How do we get in?'

William heaved himself out of the driver seat and dug in his battered tweed jacket to produce a large ring of keys from one of his many pockets. He lumbered around to the back of the vehicle to let the dogs jump out, then went round to the passenger door to open it for Vivian who was bent double repacking her substantial handbag, which had landed upside-down when it fell. The dogs charged back down the driveway, then skidded to a cautious halt as one of the stags appeared on the far side of the cattle grid to stare curiously at the car. It lowered its well-antlered head to scrutinise them and Odette nervously danced sideways, poised to bolt if necessary. Buster stood his ground but didn't bark. The animals studied each other, then the stag nodded gracefully on its way and Buster went to join Odette. William, who had been watching with his brows drawn together, relaxed and turned back towards the car.

'It *is* baronial, isn't it? Suits me, I think. I like big places. Collected the keys from Butler yesterday. The dogs should be fine, I don't think they'll cross the cattle grid and there's a six-foot steel fence in the hedges to keep the deer out, so they can explore where they want.'

He offered an enormous hand to Vivian as she sat up, slightly pink from the bending. Tall and generously-rounded as she was, she looked small next to him as he helped her out, shooting one of her lovely smiles into his face as he did, and he smiled back involuntarily.

Edge and Donald exchanged the briefest of glances. Vivian had been her best friend since childhood, and her relationship with William had been a little strained lately. Edge's glance said *that's better*, and his was *told you so*.

William, always alert to atmosphere, looked across but said only 'Brace yourself for the main hall, it's a Bambi graveyard. Just follow me and we'll make a dash through to the library. Donald, pal, it's largely up to you. Right now it is pure depressing. I want you to put your atmospheric hat on.'

'I've never done a Gothic set.' Donald's eyes gleamed as he stared upwards at the sprawling house. 'But aye, big man, worth the trip, just for the challenge.'

—ele—

'Colonel Mustard, in the library, with a blunt instrument. You don't need me, William. This room scripts itself. You even have a couple of hideous Art Deco bronze statuettes to hand as weapons.' Edge turned slowly on her heel to examine the musty gloomy library with its floor-to-ceiling bookshelves crammed with leather-backed books. She went over to the nearest rack to pull a book free, with some difficulty. 'Swollen with damp. What a *shame*, this room must have been lovely in its day. It's freezing! What happened to your aunt?'

'There wasn't one, he was a die-hard misogynist, didn't give a toss for family. Remember that WC Fields quote about women being like elephants: interesting, but you wouldn't want to own one? That was my uncle to a T. He certainly found women interesting, and he had some wild parties here back in the days when he was making money hand over fist. There's no wonder there's not much left; champagne flowed like water, nothing but the best, wall-to-wall loose lovelies. A great role model for a growing lad.' He looked round nostalgically. 'I hate seeing the place like this, collapsing in on itself.'

'I can't see you being able to move here yourself.' Donald was using a laser tape measure and jotting the results in his notebook. 'It would cost every penny you've ever earned in royalties to put it right.'

'And more.' William, a successful but not best-selling SF author, was slightly regretful. 'But I can't sell it as it stands. Butler says if anyone is injured by any of the traps I'd be liable, so there's no *giving* it away either. The Foundation won't take it unless I make it safe, and that'll cost a packet. Only alternative is to keep it, and, as you say, let it fall into extremely expensive picturesque ruin. So what do you think about a murder weekend? As soon as possible, before the weather gets too bad and the place turns into a complete icebox.' He shot a disgruntled look at the library fireplace, where the fire he had lit was smouldering sullenly. 'If Vivian's prepared to cook, at least the food will be good.'

Edge raised her eyebrows. 'I thought you said the kitchen was horrendous?'

Vivian nodded vigorously. 'Oh, it is. The oldest and biggest range you ever saw. And no fridge, just a still room next to the scullery, which would make a wonderful pantry. But it's absolutely enormous. We could rent a commercial stove and a few freezers and fridges and still have enough room to dance reels, trust me. And the guests would be mucking in and helping themselves, so I wouldn't be doing three full meals a day. It *could* be fun.'

'Oh, it could be excellent. Not terribly cosy, but in summer you wouldn't need more than three jerseys to fight off hypothermia,' Edge said drily. 'Why not go for a writer's workshop, William? You said that place you were at last week cost a fortune, and that would be a week or a fortnight at a time, much more money. You could stick with a murder theme, invite thriller writers?'

'I don't think anyone would stay longer than a weekend,' William said frankly, and gestured generally round the gloomy library. 'Would you? We'd have to stay longer as well, remember. No thanks.'

'Mmm. I'm thinking that for a really good murder weekend you'll need actors to keep it moving along, and that would cost a fair bit.'

'And dingy is all very well, but for guests paying through the nose, you'll need good sets and that costs too.' Donald cast a final glance at an ominously dark shadow on the ceiling and looked across. 'Creaking hinges and fake cobwebs, at the very least. Addams family style, or more subtle creeping horror?'

William's eyes brightened. 'Addams family! I hadn't even thought of that. Edge would make a good Morticia and you could be Gomez, dance with all the female guests.'

'I was joking,' Donald said resignedly. 'And you are certainly not pimping me out to women on the prowl for adventure. Edge won't permit it. She's shatteringly possessive.'

Edge smiled across at him. 'It's a good cause, Donald. You can dance with the scarier ones, I really won't mind. William will have to take care of the pretty ones.'

William snorted. 'I expect them to take care of each other. Actors and expensive sets, though, that's not going to leave much over for the rates and taxes. Do you think a writing retreat *would* work? The place I stayed had a phenomenal library, all mod cons, and top food. We can't offer that here.'

'But you *are* offering tons of atmosphere, especially if Donald tweaks it up a bit. More to the point, a bunch of writers who specialize in thrillers would be pretty good at finding those booby-traps for you, and they'd enjoy themselves in the process.'

'That's actually not a bad plan. And it *is* a great atmosphere, a sight more evocative than the place I tried. You could have something.'

'How's the electricity supply?' Edge grimaced involuntarily as she glanced up at the dim chandelier. 'And you'd need Wi-Fi because you're not going to get any writers here unless they can plug in to their life-support systems.'

'Dodgy.' William admitted. 'There's no signal here at all, it's a complete dead spot. Look at your mobile phone, you'll see. Still, that's fixable. I'm pretty sure we could sort out a piggyback signal of some kind. Donald, what do you think?' He looked around for the other, who was frowning over his notebook. 'What are you doing?'

'I'm puzzled. I was re-checking my measurements. There's a gap between the drawing room and this room.'

William nodded, impressed. 'You're good. Aye, there is. A hidden room. My uncle thought it was undetectable. I'll show you later. What,' he repeated, 'do you think?'

Vivian rubbed her arms and moved closer to the sullen fire. 'This horrible fire hasn't stopped smoking and the room hasn't warmed up one *iota* since you lit it. No relaxed evenings chatting in the library, that's a given. You couldn't ask much for your workshops. Would it be worth the work?'

'Ten bedrooms, that leaves eight for guests.' William did a brief mental calculation. 'Even at half what I paid for that place I went to, it would help. I could ask that much. I mean, it's very grand, people would like that.'

Donald put back the book he had pulled from the library shelves and fastidiously wiped his fingers on a dusty cushion. 'It *was* very grand. That was a first edition but it's falling apart.' He glanced up at the tiered shelves of books. 'If the musty smell in here is anything to go by, they'll all be the same.'

'Okay, so they're slightly foxed.' William, taller than most men, made a long arm to tug on a book higher up and looked dismayed as the spine came away in his fingers.

'Foxed?' Edge spluttered with laughter. 'Try buffaloed. *Water*-buffaloed! I'm sorry, William, but the books are past saving.'

'Thank you, Mrs Cameron, for underlining the obvious.' William looked round the library wistfully and sat heavily on one of the leather Chesterfields, twins to the ones in his bungalow at the Lawns. 'This used to be the best room in the house. I can't think what my uncle was doing, letting it get so neglected. He loved books.'

'You did tell us he was pretty frail by the end,' Edge said fairly as she cautiously perched on the arm of the Chesterfield. 'When you were here before did you look around? Is the rest of the place in the same condition?'

'I had a look when I went off to hunt for a loo,' Donald put in sardonically. 'Had to go upstairs in the end. The rooms are incredibly old-fashioned, and the walls are splotchy and stained. The damp problem in winter must be horrendous.'

'Ah.' William abruptly looked a bit guilty. 'Glad you made it back. I should have warned you, one of the bathrooms has a booby trap. Whatever you do, if you go into the one on the far right, do *not* touch the red switch on the wall outside. It was the most laddish of all his pranks: the idea is when you heard someone inside you flipped the switch, they finish their business, walk towards the door and whoosh.'

'*Whoosh*?' Donald stared at him. 'The toilet explodes?'

'No.' William snorted with sudden laughter. 'The floor opens. He was a bit addicted to slides, and this one shoots you out of the house altogether, into the hydrangeas. You wouldn't want to be caught on your way in, you'd be washed out on a wave of involuntary pish.'

'Your uncle sounds quite the character.' Donald wasn't amused. 'No wonder the Foundation isn't clamouring to have the place. Not the moment when you want the bottom dropping out of your world. We disable that one.'

'Probably need to rebuild the whole bathroom to get it past modern health and safety regulations.' William sobered again. 'It all comes back to money. Again.'

'What about the fortune?' Vivian swivelled to present her hips to the sullen fire.

William lifted his heavy shoulders in his familiar shrug. 'He told me not long before he died that there was a fortune hidden here,' he told Donald and Edge. 'He was a bit gaga by then, and living in the past. If there's anything hidden at all, we're probably talking a few thousand pounds in a suitcase. There's precious little in his bank accounts, royalties on his inventions dropped off sharply since his heyday. I did look in the hidden room when Vivian and I were here last week with Butler, since that was the obvious place for it, but there was nothing.'

Donald looked disappointed. 'Unless you can find that fortune and it runs to serious money, you have to ken the clock's ticking on it even being habitable.'

William growled in frustration. 'So what the hell *do* I do? Return the keys to Butler, and still be stuck with the rates and taxes, which are not shy? Sell it as it stands with an indemnity clause which may or may not hold in the face of a serious accident? The other option is to make it safe for the Foundation, and I wouldn't know where to start. I thought Butler would have a copy of the house-plans, with every trap marked, but he says not. I'm beginning to think Edge may have hit on something with a writer's retreat. Even if I only charge expenses, we could challenge the writers to find the traps. I agree the bathroom one would have to be disabled, but some are harmless, just alarming.'

'Show us one then, go on.' Donald's blue eyes were bright with interest. 'Is one of the books a Jack-in-the-box?'

'Ha.' William heaved himself back to his feet. 'You'll love this.' He stumped across the room, peering at spines of books, then gave a grunt of satisfaction and prodded at one with his stick. There was a click and a section of the bookshelf swung open. He nodded at Donald. 'Hold that open.'

Donald put his hand on the door obediently, peering into the Stygian darkness beyond. 'The missing room. It's not much of a trick, though—oi!'

The door twitched out of his fingers and slammed hollowly back into place. At the same time the door to the hall swung shut with an ominous click as it locked, and an icy draught swept the room as the flames died in the fireplace. Within seconds the coals were as dark as though they had never been lit.

'My uncle never did like people poking round on their own,' William remarked with satisfaction. 'If you nip straight into the hidden room and shut the door, nothing happens. Hold it open too long, and you trigger the trap. There was a buzzer in his room which let him know when it was found, so he could come unlock the main door. He used to tell guests the library was haunted. That's probably why it got so neglected, the cleaners likely believed him.'

Edge hugged herself and shivered. 'I hate to be the one to say this, William, but he's not going to be coming to let us out. At least, I hope he's not, or I will go into strong hysterics. You'd better have a back-up plan.'

'Of course I do.' He looked patient. 'I press this bit of moulding, and hey presto.'

Vivian looked at the library door, which stayed stubbornly shut. 'So presto it. I want the loo, a coffee, and something to eat.'

William pressed the rosette in the moulding again, frowning. 'I'm sure it was this one. Maybe this one?' He tried a few others, higher and lower. The door didn't budge.

'Didn't you see how it was done last time?' Edge asked Vivian, who shook her head.

'Stuart Butler went outside for a cigarette, and I grabbed the chance to go out with him and defrost in the sun. William said he wouldn't be long. I was to come find him if he screamed, or didn't reappear. '

William shrugged. 'I told Butler how it worked, which book to press in case, but I didn't trigger it last time. I went straight in. There's a handle on the inside of the hidden room for getting out.'

'How did it get so cold in here?' Donald crossed to the fire and hunkered down to look at the coals. 'No wonder this didn't burn well, if it's jiggered. Can I light it again, or will it not light again until the door opens?'

'Click your lighter,' William ordered and moved slightly sideways to toe an almost invisible mark on the hearth. Donald's lighter flared, and the flames climbed again to their previous listless height, eddying in the insistent breeze. 'Looks like that's still all we'll get, it used to be a real blaze. The smoking was probably cobwebs and dust. Blast the old man and his old broken traps!'

'You're as bad as he was, deliberately triggering it.' Vivian moved resignedly back to the fireplace. 'Now it's *really* perishing in here!'

'Concealed cold air vents. They close again when the door opens. I can't switch them off separately. Damn!'

'This rosette, was it?' Donald peered at the first one William had tried, jiggled it slightly with his thumb, and pushed hard. The library door to the passage clicked and the chilly draught stopped instantly. Edge lunged over to pull the door wide with a gasp of relief.

Printed in Great Britain
by Amazon

58544228R00081